Contents

Into the Darkness

An Introduction

My first introduction to the Gothic Tradition was attempting to read *Wuthering Heights* when I was nine. I was far too young to understand what was going on and I think I gave up after ten pages. This book became my Everest. It wasn't until I was fifteen and had ploughed through the Russian masters that I believed I could take on Emily Brontë a second time. I devoured *Wuthering Heights* and my outlook on literature changed. The intensity of the fear, love, atmosphere, environment, and characters Brontë created remain my benchmark for a great read. Imagine then my joy when we began studying the Gothic Tradition in college and good old WH was a set text. When I delved deeper into the book, behind the black type and into the real *meaning* of it, I knew I, one day, wanted to celebrate that in print. I give you then, a decade later, *The New Gothic*.

In a very small nutshell, as it's too vast an area for just this introduction, the Gothic in literature traces its origins back to one novel, *The Castle of Otranto* by Horace Walpole, published in 1764. It's a short novel involving a ramshackle castle, mysterious deaths, ghostly happenings, and heightened emotions, predominantly love and fear, which border on the violent. These became the foundations of a literary style that would go on to inspire authors such as Mary Shelley, Edgar Allan Poe, Daphne du Maurier, M. R. James, Matthew Lewis, Bram Stoker, the Brontës, Ann Radcliffe, and Susan Hill, and even spawn a parody of the style from Jane Austen.

There is a level of emotion in the Gothic that doesn't exist in pure horror and I believe that is an important distinction to mention. To me, horror is external where the Gothic is internal. In horror, the ghost really is at the window. In the Gothic, the ghost is a manifestation of the narrator's internal fear or his all-consuming love for the deceased. The stories I have collected in this anthology epitomise the Gothic in different ways and some will leave a lasting impression on you.

The New Gothic was the first Stone Skin Press anthology to call for open submissions. I firmly believe this was the best decision for this book. I made my (slow) way through hundreds of short stories; the standard was extremely high and I considered each one carefully. The brief was simple — write a story that celebrates the Gothic Tradition. It could be set anywhere and at any time, and that's what I got.

Jesse Bullington and S. J. Chambers team up for their contribution to the Gothic. "Dive in Me" tells of three friends trying to escape the summer heat but ends with a visual that I still can't get out of my head. Bullington and Chambers evoke the sweltering heat and urban degeneration of the area with a masterful use of dialect and slang. Subtle terror pervades the small town visited by the narrator of "The Debt Collector" by Fi Michell. Although he quickly discovers there is a vampire in the village, the extent of the vampire's influence makes for a disturbing revelation. The story is a slow burn with an atmosphere reminiscent of Susan Hill's *The Woman in Black*. "The Death Bell" by Laura Ellen Joyce involves two connected stories, beautifully told, one tale of a woman visited by her nephew, one tale of a couple on a first date. The gradual build-up to the shocking denouement is deliciously torturous.

Richard Dansky's "A Meeting in the Devil's House" embraces the Southern Gothic and begins with one of my favourite tropes; a mysterious meeting between strangers in a remote house. With Lovecraftian influences, the house and its two unwitting visitors are pulled into a situation they can't possibly comprehend or escape. Steve Dempsey takes the Gothic to the snowy climes of North America in "No Substitute." It employs the classic framework narrative to great effect, taking the reader in one moment from an opulent dining room then to a ship wrecking in freezing waters. In "Reading the Signs," Ramsey Campbell, a master of the form who needs no introduction, turns a drive in the country into a nightmarish experience. I don't think I'll ever look at seatbelts the same way. Read it, you'll see what I mean.

In "The Boy by the Gate," Dmetri Kakmi gives us a beautifully classic tale of a disappearance and a friend who goes searching. Kakmi begins his story, as we all would, safely around a fire with friends, but what follows takes us far from this warmth. In "Viola's Second Husband," Sean Logan shows the deterioration of a grandfather through the eyes of his grandson, but as the man gets weaker, the titular Viola seems more full of life than ever.

In "The Devil in a Hole," Mason Wild easily evokes the craggy, sun-kissed landscape of the Ardèche Valley in France with a tale that both disgusts and delights. His "cadaver man" is one of the most original characters I have seen in a long time and Wild's use of scripture and metaphor adds great depth to such a short story. In "The Whipping Boy," Damien Kelly brings the bleak desolation of a remote village in Ireland to the fore. He shows us all one of our worst nightmares — a summer stuck with your bully, but our protagonist discovers that getting your own back has a price.

Beautiful Lovecraftian prose from Phil Reeves abounds in "The Vault of Artemas Smith" and instantly places the reader into the dank vaults beneath a demolished house. In true Gothic style however, our narrator and his unfortunate friend are not the only things lurking in the dark passages. Lastly, "The Fall of the Old Faith" was one of the first submissions for *The New Gothic* and remains one of my favourite stories, not just in this anthology but any. Ed Martin's appreciation of the old masters, M. R. James and Edgar Allan Poe, is obvious in his prose and structure. The sound of a door creaking open on a forested hill thrusts our narrator, and us along with him, into a chilling sequence of events from which nobody will escape unscathed.

Twelve stories from twelve master storytellers, each with a unique take on the tradition. I have not gone into great detail in what the Gothic is about in a wide context; it would take too long and it's a subject that has been written about extensively over the last two hundred years. I have talked about what the Gothic tradition means to me, the authors I adore, how I came to fall in love with it, and how I came to compile this anthology. I hope you enjoy these tales as much as I have. This literary style is everywhere and there are always new stories or novels popping up. There is still much to discover in the darkness but, with the Gothic, you don't get a flashlight, you get a flickering candle and it's windy out there.

Beth K Lewis
November 2013

Dive in Me

Jesse Bullington and S. J. Chambers

The girls were a gang of three: a triad, a triumvirate, or what have you. Like the Gorgons and Moirai before them, they never made a move or decision separately. So when Spring was missing from their usual hook-up spot in the kudzu-veiled lot behind the Hoggly Woggly one Saturday morning, the gang was thrown into a state of chaos.

"Where the fuck is she?"

"You don't think she got busted last night, do you?"

Gina paused to consider this, because it was a real possibility. They had been in the alley behind the skating rink throwing bricks at streetlights until the girls were broken up by crescendoing sirens and red and blue illuminations. In such desperate if not rare instances, they would all separate and regroup later.

"Nah, if she got bagged, we'd hear about it right?" Gina sat on a vine-cushioned log.

"Um, how?"

Gina pointed at the nearby pay phone. "You get a phone call, don't you?"

"Uh, yeah, to call someone that can bail you out. She knows we can't bail a dog out of the pound, much less her skanky bitch ass from jail." Moira seemed pleased with this comparison and either ignored or didn't notice Gina's growing concern. Bullshitting nosy cops was one thing, and actually running from them not unheard of, but so far none of them had actually been caught.

"Okay, well, she'd call her house, then," said Gina. "If she's not home, Hughes'll know where she's at."

Gina dug in the cavernous pockets of her baggy jeans for a quarter as she picked up the pay phone with her other hand, and so she didn't see what was coating it until her fingers closed on cold, slimy slickness. She yelped and pulled her hand back, quickly looking around to make sure Moira hadn't seen her chickenshit reaction before she took a better look at the nastiness tangled around the phone. The parking lot and pumps were mostly empty, and, turning her attention back to the now-dangling receiver, she saw dripping duckweed wrapped all around the black plastic phone. Wiping her hand on her jeans, Gina smiled — that wasn't a bad gag, winding some shit around a phone. She would've used poison ivy, personally, and limited its use to the earpiece. That wouldn't provoke the same immediate revulsion, but whatever dumbass picked it up would grind the ivy into their ear before they noticed what was up. Tearing off the duckweed, she rang Spring's house.

"Yeah?" Hughes sounded groggy. It was, after all, noon o' clock, so Gina had either woke him up or caught him in the middle of his morning burn. He was Spring's boyfriend, and was a lot older than the girls. He claimed to be sixteen, but Moira suspected he was really twenty-one, because he always had booze and, more favorably, weed. She could picture him in a shredded Pearl Jam shirt and Superman boxers, his stringy red hair screening his bloodshot eyes.

"Hughes! Where the fuck is Spring? She was supposed to meet us behind Hoggy Wogs."

"I dunno… she was supposed to be crashing at your house."

"No, she wasn't," said Gina. Moira motioned at her that she was going inside to get a soda.

"Look, she told me she was sleeping over with you lezzers, and y'all were hitting the sinks today. That's all I know. Now fuck off." The line went dead.

After hanging up the phone, Gina walked into the store to find Moira flipping through an issue of *CREEM*.

"What'd he say?" she asked without looking up.

"God," said Gina. "He's so fucking gross."

"Oh, I dunno. I think he's cute. Kind of has a Layne Staley thing going, you know?" Moira turned the magazine around to show Gina an Alice in Chains spread to prove her case.

"I'm sure he'd cream himself to hear that, Moira." Moira frogged Gina in the arm. "Jesus, ow! Well, whatever, according to his stoned ass, Spring never came home last night, and is supposed to be hitting the sinks with us today."

"We didn't talk about swimming."

"You think there was some mix-up, and she's waiting for us at one of the holes?"

"Could be. I guess we could check out the usual suspects, if your brother will pick us up."

Gina had just dropped her last quarter in the phone when a long, distended shadow fell over the wall in front of her.

"Damn, but that is one sorry lookin' bitch!" The familiar voice was right behind Gina, making her jump. "Don't tell me your pimp lets you out of the crack house looking like that."

"Where've you been?" asked Gina, trying not to let her relief show as she wiped her sweaty bangs from her forehead and turned to Spring. "We've been looking all over, and Hughes said —"

"Suicide Sinks." Spring offered up the jagged grin of a girl who had never been to the dentist and was in general a hot fucking mess. She was covered in sweat, XXL flannel and parachute jeans not being the breeziest summertime attire. Her fading Kool-Aid dye job shed splotches of color on her shoulders and the parking lot. "It took all night, but I found those bitches!"

All the relief Gina felt at finding Spring curdled in her stomach. When the other two had talked about finding the fabled sinkholes, she had gone along with it, because of course she had, but the possibility of the place really existing, much less their discovering its location, had never seriously darkened her imagination.

"Who were you calling?" asked Spring.

"Dave." When Spring wrinkled her nose, Gina said, "He sucks, but he'll drive us anywhere we wanna go, so long as Moira's with us. Unless Prince Charming in Chains got his license un-suspended?"

"Don't matter," said Spring. "We're walking — this is top secret, for skanks' eyes only."

"Oh."

"Moira inside?" Gina nodded. "You got any smokes?"

Gina nodded again. "Yeah, I lifted some Dorals from my stepdad, but they have to last all weekend. See if you can lift a pack from inside, or Hey Mister that redneck."

"That dude looks like a bitch — what kinda self-respecting good old boy drives a Kia? I'll try my luck in the pigsty, and get Moira to buy some jerky. It's a long walk to the Sinks from here; I've been running back here all fuckin' morning. And you Hey Mister that pussy anyway, you can't have too many coffin nails, Gina, not before Suicide."

Gina eyed Spring's damp hair and clothes. Nobody knew where Suicide Sinks were, if they even existed, and all of the usual swimmable sinkholes were at least a twenty-minute drive away — no way Spring was running that route. Gina also wondered if it wasn't just sweat from the balls-hot morning. "Did you… you went swimming there last night?"

"I wouldn't dive in without you and Moira! We're all going in together."

Great, Gina thought. Then Spring was gone, her heavy jeans swishing as she darted into the store. Gina looked forlornly after her. It wasn't even noon yet and was hotter than hell, the leaves of the kudzu on the gas station wall dripping in the still, muggy air. Walking anywhere in this heat sounded r-tarded, and the promise of a swim at the end actually made it worse, for a change.

♦

Anything that makes you feel alive can't be all that bad. This was the mantra that Gina used to justify all sorts of dubious adventures with Moira and Spring, the other two being decidedly less cautious than she when it came to, well, everything. Gina was the brains, and the other two were the balls — not that she would ever voice such a sentiment, since they were also both a lot punchier than her. This plot, however, didn't give her the same queasy-awesome thrill as smashing streetlights or boosting shitty jewelry from Claire's, though the threat of police or pissed-off parents was a lot smaller. This plan filled her with dread. For the first hour, she smoked cig after cig, trying to come up with a plan on how to either talk them out of it or get herself out of it. She was just waiting for an opening, but Moira's enthusiasm kept common sense out of the conversation as they followed Spring until the cracked sidewalks gave way to the long grass that bordered the old highway leading out of town.

"C'mon," Moira said. "Tell us!"

"Fine," Spring said. "But it's nothing major. Just don't tell Hughes, you know how he gets."

Moira gave Gina a meaningful look. *How he gets?*

"When you bitches dipped out on me, I barely got away from the cops. Some Woodvillians were leaving the skate rink, and I bummed a lift with them. Couple of dirtbags and this spooky fat girl. They were going to hop a fence at some motel and go swimming, but, halfway there, Thick Girl mumbled something about Suicide Sinks. These goons knew where it was, and, even though they gave me a hard time, I talked 'em into taking me out there instead of hitting the motel pool. Those dirtbags took me right to it!"

"How do you know it was really Suicide?" said Moira. "And not some random redneck mud puddle?"

"I could feel it, right? Like, a sick sense."

"Sixth," said Gina. "Sixth sense."

"Sick Sense sounds better," said Moira. "That'd be a cool band name."

Typical stupid Florida woods bordered the half-dead highway out there, with rotten old shotgun shacks set back in the pines. The houses were mostly abandoned, and what little traffic passed them on the road consisted of semis and company trucks for the chemical plant. At last they reached a particular overgrown dirt road that looked the same as every other turnoff they'd passed — barred by barbwire and flanked by flapping *No Trespassing* signs stapled to trees. Spring glanced up and down the highway and, seeing the coast was clear, ducked under the wire and booked it down the grassy track. This was a familiar ritual, and Gina and Moira were right behind her, the triad not slowing until they were well out of sight of the highway, their clothes instantly sopping from the sprint.

"I heard Hawk Point was condemned," said Gina once she'd caught her breath enough to light a cigarette. Talking about stuff with her friends always made it less creepy, more laughable.

"Huh?" Moira found a stick to break in half and toss back into the woods.

"Back before they called 'em Suicide Sinks, this must have been Hawk Point," said Gina.

"Sounds like an ancient Indian burial ground," said Moira, then added. "Ba-chawk!"

"Shut up," said Spring and Gina simultaneously. Gina was secretly relieved to have Spring on her side. Usually she and Moira made a constant racket, even — especially — when they were doing something furtive.

"Hawk Point was one of the first suburbs this far out of town," said Gina. "Quiet place to raise a family, good property values, and not too close to all the rednecks and *black people*." This last she said in a hushed, scared old-white-lady voice. "But then something happened."

"Dun dun *dunh!*" said Moira.

"You guys know about sinkholes, how they'll just…" Gina gulped, the air thick in her throat. "*Devour* whatever they open up under. A whole house, yard and all, isn't unheard of."

"Yeah?" said Moira, snatching Gina's cigarette from where it languished between her fingers. "So?"

Gina scowled at Moira. "So the fact is a sinkhole opened under *every* house in Hawk Point, every single one. *At the same time.* Middle of the night, when everyone was at home in bed, the ground just… swallowed them up. Houses, cars, playgrounds. *Dog* houses. Nobody got out. Geologically speaking, the incident was a phenomenon."

The only sound was the girls' jeans scratching against the grass that sprouted in the middle of the road and the droning of insects, and then Moira said, "I call bullshit, dude. No way a bunch of picket fencers got sucked into sinks without everybody in town knowing about it."

"This was years and years ago," said Gina. "And everyone *does* know about it, right? I mean, who hasn't heard of Suicide Sinks? That's why they don't let people come back here, because the ground's unstable."

The dirt track they were walking joined a narrow paved road, but one so ancient the ragged blacktop was mostly hidden under countless generations of rotting vegetation.

"The whole place is fucked, and not just because of the sinks," Gina continued as they veered onto this new path. "Before they got sunk, those entitled motherfuckers who lived here were so lazy that they poured oil and all their trash into the river rather than drive to the dump. Shit like that."

"Yeah," Spring said. "I asked Ms. Hannah about it. She said it was because it was close to the river and caverns that the ground was probably already eroded and too soft, or whatever, and the developers fucked it up with, uh, putting in a sewer thing or something."

"Ha-ha, yeah, they pissed Earth off and she opened up and ate them all!" Moira goosed Spring, and snatched her hand back. "Damn, dude, you're freezing! You sure you're not sick, fever-dreamed all this shit up?"

Gina looked at the sweat beading off of Spring's flushed face. She didn't *look* sick, and they were all pretty sweaty. A raptor soared overhead and landed in a pine tree.

"I'd kill to be freezing right about now," Spring said. "You must've been nipping from Hughes's stash again, Moira, or maybe you got frostbite from fingering Gina's frigid snatch."

"Bleh! Anywho, I bet that shit is nasty," said Moira. "The sinks, I mean, not your 'gina, Gina. I'm sure you're a very clean girl. Spotless, even."

Gina ignored them. "They would have to put up signs. No way this is the right place, not without more signs."

"Uh, you mean like all the signs we passed?" Spring shook her head, then dramatically swept her arm to the side. "Or that one over there?"

"No fucking way," Moira whispered. Then, substantially louder: "No fucking way!"

The ornamental boulder wore a mantle of kudzu vines, the thickly etched letters on its face outlined in moss. At its base, shredded warning signs mixed with the dead leaves like offerings at an altar. Moira did a victory pogo while Spring smugly watched Gina. *Hawk Point*, it read.

Beyond the sign was a much more serious barricade than the wire they had ducked back on the highway, but the galvanized gate was built to keep out cars, not juvenile delinquents on foot. As soon as she landed on the age-warped blacktop on the far side of the gate, Gina felt her stomach twist up, like she was getting cramps. It seemed louder on this side, the bug noises echoing through the hollows, Moira's braying voice ricocheting off the pines.

"Whatever happened out here, they were fucking with sacred ground," said Gina, and almost meant it. Remembering Moira's crack from before, she said. "Ain't there Miccosukee burial mounds around here? Maybe we shouldn't be fucking around here either."

"Maybe you shouldn't be such a puss," Moira said, sticking her tongue between her fingers in retort to the bird Gina was shooting her.

"It doesn't look that bad," Spring said once Moira and Gina had settled down. "You'll see."

They marched on. Spring retrieved a fallen branch to bat down the sticky banana spider webs that frequently blocked their path, and Moira scoured the ground for pine cones to kick. Gina continued to smoke and ruminate. As if Hawk Point's history wasn't disturbing enough, there was the reason everyone called this place Suicide Sinks. It wasn't that people came here when they were Kurt-minded, but just that every once in a while, some kid would go missing, and, after several weeks of searching, they'd find him floating down the river thirty miles from anywhere he was supposed to be. Reports on these dumbasses would show they hadn't been murdered or messed with, just drowned somehow, and eventually they figured out with maps or sonar or something that they all must have tried to dive the Suicide Sinks and failed. Like a lot of sinks, these were supposed to be connected by underwater caves.

And of course there were plenty of kids who never showed up in the river, or anywhere, period. Gina couldn't stop imagining herself swimming into some bloated corpse's arms and being drowned in its empty embrace… until the image became her and Moira and Spring floating lifelessly among all the other divers over waterlogged houses.

"Listen," Gina said. "I don't think I can dive with you, Spring."

"Why?" Spring asked.

"I suck at diving, man. I can't hold my breath for shit, and we've been doing all this walking and smoking and…" She hesitated. "And if you two dumbasses get in a jam, I can go for help."

Moira began to splutter, but Spring held up her cigarette to Moira's mouth. "Put a butt in it, Moira." Moira took the cig and puffed, winking at Gina through exhaled smoke.

Spring stared at Gina for awhile as they all continued walking.

"You don't think we can handle it?" Spring's voice was odd. Gina couldn't tell if she was concerned or contemptible of the assumed doubt or what.

"I know you can hold your breath forever. You I'm not worried about —" Gina darted her eyes at Moira. "Moira probably could too. It's just you don't know what's down there. No one does. Anyone who's ever dived there has never come back. That doesn't concern you?"

"Pfth. Tons of people do it. Those dumbasses from last night did it right in front of me, no problem. Anyone who doesn't come back drowns because they were either too fucked up, or just bullshit swimmers."

"What about that one dude," asked Moira. "The pro diver, or whatever, they found in the river last summer?"

Spring cut Moira a hellish look, and Moira just shrugged and lit another smoke with the dying ember of the previous butt.

"He was probably bullshit, too. I am not bullshit, and I'm not afraid to dive."

For the first time in their friendship, Spring seemed upset. Tears welled in her eyes. The intensity on her friend's face made Gina uncomfortable. She knew swimming was Spring's thing — everyone had a thing: Gina rocked math and the drums, and Moira was awesome at reconstructing clothes and doing hair. Spring *was* a killer swimmer, and a diver, too, but this… this emotion, this fear on Spring's face, was totally out of character, and it creeped Gina out. She had a notion, a fluttery feeling in her gut, that not just diving, but *surviving*, Suicide Sinks was so important to Spring that nothing, not a damn thing, could talk her out of it now. Their march had already gone too far to be deterred, and now Moira and Gina's fates were tied into these stupid sinkholes, also.

The girls stopped walking, and the heaviness of the heat and the insect thrumming of the forest weighed down on them, palpable, relentless. Gina sighed it off and began to air guitar the opening bass riff to Nirvana's "Dive."

Moira giggled and put her arm around Spring as she began to sing an altered version of the chorus: "Dive! Dive! Dive! Dive with me!"

Gina joined in, making Spring laugh and put her arm around Gina, who flinched. Moira had been right: Spring was cold, colder than Wakulla Springs in the middle of January, but, as with a dip in any winter spring, after the initial shock, you could barely feel the chill. Gina savored the coolness against her skin, and the girls sang the rest of their march down the abandoned road of the legendary housing development.

◆

When the first house appeared, they all stopped and stared.

"So not all the houses got sunk, huh?" Moira looked over Spring's head at Gina. "Told you that story was shit."

Gina should have been relieved to see such irrefutable proof that all the stories about Hawk Point were bullshit, that of course a whole neighborhood didn't fall into the earth. Yet the dilapidated, boarded-up ranch house failed to give any comfort whatsoever, the scaling paint on its face reminding her of a peeling poison-ivy rash. Gaunt cypress saplings poked out of the jungle where its front yard had been, and, as they came abreast with it, they saw a live oak had pitched through the side wall.

"If you knew, why didn't you say?" Gina asked Spring.

She shrugged. "You were half-right, anyway, about them condemning the place. Ground must have been too soft to even bring in machinery to tear these wrecks down."

"We are so going in there," said Moira, already moving up the driveway when Spring grabbed her arm.

"After. First we do the sinks, then you can play house. C'mon," said Spring, hooking Gina with her other cold-ass arm and dragging both girls away from the house.

Moira cackled, then pointed at another house that was coming into sight through the trees. "Dibs on that one. You bring housewarming swag, I *might* let your sorry asses come over for tea and croquet."

"Then I get the next one," said Gina, trying to force herself into the spirit of things. It had worked before — sometimes she just needed to push herself a little to find the fun. Soon enough, though, she regretted claiming an estate sight unseen.

At the end of the third driveway of Hawk Point, all that remained of the house were a few foundations poking up on the rim. They looked like the gravestones Gina had been too chickenshit to spray paint a few weeks ago. Beyond them, beneath them, the sink waited.

Unlike most sinkholes the girls swam in, there was little greenery flanking the sides of the pit, just red clay. It was roughly circular, maybe fifty feet across, and couldn't be more than a ten-foot drop down to the water, but Gina felt dizzy looking over the broken driveway's concrete lip. The water was crystal clear, and, at the right angle, you could see — way, way down — the house's roof, with waterweed columns rising from its moldering shingles. Despite herself, Gina leaned the slightest bit further, looking for the cave that supposedly linked this sink to others in the area, and eventually the river, but the sheer walls of the pit were too dark to tell.

Two hands hit Gina in the small of her back, hard. She stumbled forward but caught herself, and there was a desperate moment where her breath caught and her stomach lurched and her head went light, the toes of her boots rocking on the rough edge of the driveway, and she was going to balance herself, she was...

No. She was too scared to move, and, as if she were a helpless prisoner in her own body, she felt her weight shift, felt the driveway betray her, offering her up as a sacrifice as she toppled —

Spring grabbed her shirt and jerked her backwards, and Gina collapsed onto the driveway. The sounds of Moira laughing and Spring cursing at Moira were muffled by the sudden ringing that filled Gina's ears. When she caught her breath, she faked a laugh, but even she could tell it sounded off and desperate. Another Doral didn't help, but it did give her something to flick at Moira once she stopped shaking enough to properly aim it.

"Oh dude, what a fuckin' waste!" Moira had sidestepped the missile, and stared forlornly down to where it had sizzled out in the sink. "How many more do we have?"

"Last one," said Gina as Spring helped her up. "I could've cracked my head on the cement, you dumb broad."

"I wasn't really going to let you fall," said Moira. "Probably."

"We've all got to go in on our own," said Spring, by way of arbitration. "But we're all going in."

"Man, even if I wanted to, which I don't, there's no way to get out," said Gina, gesturing at the sink. "Look how steep the sides are. You'd need a rope to climb out, and I don't see any."

"Huh." Moira nodded. "There's probably one tied on a tree or something. Let's look around and see if we can find it."

"We don't need one," said Spring, but accompanied Gina anyway as she took the left side and Moira went right, inspecting the oaks and elms that were near the rim. They reconvened on the far side, where the undergrowth was even thicker.

"No rope means no rope swing," said Moira. "And no rope swing means bullllllllshit sink."

"That's probably why they call it Suicide," said Gina. "You'd have to be self-harmy jumping into a sink you couldn't get out of."

"Oh, there's a way out," said Spring slyly. "A bunch of 'em, probably, but we only need one."

"Huh?"

"Get ready, then take a deep breath and follow me," said Spring. When Gina took a step back from the sink, Spring grinned. "Don't worry, I'm not pushing you in. I told you, we all go in on our own. But first, hold your breath on three. One. Two. Three."

As soon as they all took in their lungfuls, Spring began plowing straight through the tangle of thin vines and spiky devil's walking sticks. Moira let Gina push after her, more than happy to let them clear the path a bit, then followed. Her chest had only just begun to hurt when Moira straightened up from her bent walk through the undergrowth and gasped, Spring stepping aside so Gina could join them.

They stood on the bank of a second sink, one entirely enclosed by the nearly impenetrable push of greenery. It was much smaller than the first, with cypress knees jutting out of the gently sloping bank of black mud that angled down to its mirror-still surface. Instead of a nauseating depth, this sink looked to be barely a dozen feet deep and narrow, before it curved into algae-softened rock.

"Oh no," said Gina. "Oh fuck no. Spring, there's no way you can do this. No fucking way."

"You held your breath the whole way," said Spring. "I was listening. And if a smokestack like you can do it, then —"

"Walking a few feet in the woods with my breath held is a lot fucking different than swimming through a cave! It'll be dark down there; you won't see where you're going."

"There's a rope," countered Spring, her bemusement at Gina's reaction fermenting into something nastier. "It goes from one end to the other. You just grab a hold and follow it to the end."

"And if you drop it? Or if it's rotten and falls apart?"

"Then they find you in the river in a few weeks," said Moira quietly. "Dude, I don't think this is such a hot idea."

"The guys I came out here with last night did it. Twice." Spring crossed her arms. "And it was dark as shit, so they didn't even have that going for them. When you get to the end, the cave splits, and you'll be able to see the right way to go from the light. Just drop the rope and kick your way out fast. Besides, there's a spot about halfway through where the roof of the cave opens up and you can surface and breathe, then go the rest of the way."

"Man, what?" For a change, Moira looked to Gina for support. "What if those dudes didn't really swim it, but were pranking you somehow? Seeing if they could trick you into jumping in? You said it was dark, so maybe they tricked you, made it look like —"

"No," said Gina, feeling like a total dumbass for not seeing it sooner. "No, she's right. She knows."

"Huh?" Moira glanced back and forth between her friends. "How can she be sure?"

"She's sure because she already swam it," said Gina, feeling sick to her stomach. She imagined Spring squirming blindly through sunken tunnels, her breath going bad in her chest, her fingers clinging to a slimy rope tethered to the cave walls. Stupid, *stupid* goddamn Spring. "Last night, when you came out here. Those guys swam it, so you swam it after them. That's how you know."

"Half-right, as usual," said Spring smugly. "Those pussies who took me out here were too scared to get in, so I swam it myself."

The woods were loud, and something small splashed back in the first sink. The girls looked at one another. Moira spoke first, her voice heavy with doubt.

"You said you were waiting for us. Why'd you... why didn't you wait? Why'd you bullshit us about it?"

"One look at these sinks, and I knew Gina would have a heart attack if I tried it in front of her bitch ass, and that you'd be too scared to jump in, too. This way I made sure for us, for *all* of us, so we could come back and do it together without worrying."

Moira chewed her lip, and Gina followed suit. Spring had that weird frail look to her that had freaked Gina out so much before, as if maybe she wasn't quite as badass as everybody assumed. Gina felt something rich and thick — an awareness — pushing through her, almost as if her blood was congealing in her veins. All this time Gina had been psyching herself out, letting a bunch of bullshit urban legends and her imagination harsh her calm as she played tough, when all along Spring was the one who was scared. Not just scared, goddamn petrified! And of what? That her closest friends wouldn't think she was a badass unless she did something suicidally stupid?

Awareness turned to awakening, and Gina let it out, then, the wildness that only her friends could unlock in her, and the feeling of unbridled craziness was ecstatic. The undergrowth ripped at her clothes as she dashed back the way they'd come, the heat and humidity almost electric against her skin as she teetered on the edge of the first sink, almost tumbling in when she burst from the ivy and thorns. Her flannel and boots came off in a rush, before she could chicken out, and then the bra she didn't really need yet, but she left her black shirt on. Moira and Spring caught up, howling encouragement, and she stumbled out of her jeans and socks.

With a whoop, Gina launched herself clumsily into the air. She looked up breathless into the sky. The daily thunderstorms were rolling in.

And just like that Gina came back to herself, suspended in the air over the sunken house, and she screamed as the enormity of what she'd committed herself to struck her like a sucker punch. Then she fell, the walls of the sinkhole lunging up to swallow her whole. She hit the clear water and sank halfway down to the house, then kicked up, heart pinballing around her chest. Just before she surfaced she saw the black mouth of the cave set in the wall of the sink, an equally black cable floating in front of its maw like some deep sea creature's lure. Breaking the surface, she was set to beg Moira and Spring to break into a house and find some rope to haul her up when the other two girls hit the water on either side of her.

"Can't do it," Gina chattered, hating how her teeth were rattling despite the water's warmth.

Even treading water was difficult with the sodden shirt pulling her down, but Gina was reluctant to take it off, even when she noticed the other girls were skinny-dipping. Spring usually wore a bikini instead of underwear for just such occasions, but not this time, apparently. Gina's surprise at seeing them naked only distracted her from their predicament for a moment, before the horror of their situation reasserted itself. "Can't do it. Can't."

"Sure you can," said Spring. "You just…"

Then she was gone, flipping around and diving deep. She went into the cave without even bothering to grab the rope, and Gina groaned.

"This was your idea," Moira said fiercely, dog-paddling over to Gina. "I figured you knew some other way out!"

"Noooo," Gina felt herself getting sick, she was going to puke right here, but people couldn't throw up and swim at the same time, could they? She was going to drown mid-puke and —

"Easy as that!" Spring called from just above them, and Gina looked up to see Spring standing atop the buckled driveway, sleek and shining and outlined by the dirty brown clouds gathering at her back. "Hurry up, everyone out of the pool. Storm's a-comin'!"

Moira laughed and splashed Gina, who could only tread water and gape up at Spring. It had only seemed like a couple of seconds since she dived down into the cave — she must have really lost her shit for a minute there. Gina felt her cheeks flush, and wondered how many people drowned because they wigged themselves out for no reason.

"I'm next!" said Moira, because Moira was always next, and Gina felt her fear return as her friend bobbed over to the edge of the sink above the cave. "I just follow the rope, right?"

"All the way to the end, babe," said Spring. "Halfway through you come up in a cave, so take time to catch your breath there before you go the rest of the way. From there you should be able to see the light from the other cave, so just follow it out. But don't let go of the rope, just in case!"

"Be careful," said Gina, and then Moira was gone.

"I'll wait for her over at the other end, make sure she doesn't stay down too long," said Spring, and before Gina could embarrass herself by asking Spring to stay with her instead, the other girl was gone. Gina began counting, both to take her mind off the fact that she was paddling above a house that was probably full of dead people and also to see how long it took Moira to pass through. Last time Spring had bothered timing them, Gina and Moira could both hold their breath for about a minute, so even if Moira rested for five at the halfway cave she should be out in seven…

At eight minutes, Gina began to freak out.

At nine, she was almost hyperventilating.

At halfway to ten, she started screaming for Spring, Moira, the cops, anyone.

And then Moira poked her head out from behind an oak at the lip of the sink, her teeth shining even in the half-light of the brewing storm. Spring emerged from the other side of the tree, her jacked-up smile also taunting Gina. At first Gina couldn't say anything, then she didn't want to. Neither Spring nor Moira said anything, just looked down at her as the raindrops began to dimple the water and thunder echoed from back out on the highway.

"Fuck you guys," said Gina, meaning it like she'd never meant it before, and, shimmying out of the cloying shirt, she dived.

The rope was thick and slimy, but there didn't seem to be much give on it. Staring into the darkness of the cave entrance, Gina felt the sudden need to kick back up and get another lungful or a hundred, maybe beg her friends to go for help… but then their condescending smiles flashed through her mind, and, closing her eyes, Gina sunk her fingernails into the rope and pulled herself into the cave.

Every time she pulled herself forward, Gina banged a shoulder or hip on slick stone, but the walls of the cave were never there for purchase when she tried to kick herself faster along. The air in her lungs turned bad and she pushed it out, trying not to let the reality of where she was and what she was doing take hold. Her chest went from tingling to hot to a furnace, and then she felt light-headed, her limbs itched. She was going to black out.

She swam faster, letting go of the rope and opening her eyes in the hope that she could catch some glint of daylight to make for. Instead, she saw a soft glow emanating from… a TV? She had drifted into a retro living room occupied by lounging skeletons in fish-eaten board shorts and bikinis watching a busted, waterlogged television. In the middle of this family, Spring and Moira sat on the couch, their hair floating above their faces like halos. Gina gasped and swallowed water, making her body convulse against this inevitable drowning. She jetted mute screams. She didn't want to drown… She didn't even want to dive in the first place. She —

Surfaced with a gasp. Gina coughed up water and gulped the stale, moist oxygen, reveling in the way it burned her lungs. She had made it. The halfway cave.

"Gina? Is that you?"

Gina's legs and arms cramped at the sound of Moira's voice. What the fuck was she doing here? Why would she swim back in—they could have collided in the dark, or become stuck, or —

A faint light poured down with the rain pelting Gina's face, and with its illumination, she saw Moira treading water with a load. She was clinging to a vague lump of driftwood. Other than Moira and the undulating surface of the underground lake, Gina couldn't see shit.

"Ginaaaaa!" Moira shrieked, her voice echoing in the shadows.

"It's me," Gina panted, paddling closer to Moira, and, it seemed, the light. "Why'd you swim back down?"

"What? Oh, God! What's fucking happening?" Moira splashed around, struggling with her makeshift buoy. She thrust it from her body, sobbing as it bobbed further into the light. Gina saw Spring's hay-colored hair completely cleansed of its cherry-flavored dye, and then her friend's face came into sight as the body slowly rotated in the water, revealing a bluish, bloated face.

"I found her as soon as I came up here, but what the fuck — she's supposed to be up top! I saw her, she made it!" Moira's voice broke, and Gina felt the panic in her friend's voice infect her even as she looked away from the corpse, telling herself it wasn't really there. They had both just seen Spring, and she was fine. Before Gina could reflexively tell Moira it was okay, even though it definitely wasn't, something fell, splashing her in the face. Gina looked up and saw where the light was coming from: a small circle of pale light was above them, with two smaller circles of darkness limned against its border. Faces, peering down, the rain drizzling around them. Gina's eyes burned, and, rubbing them with her knuckles, she squinted up. Spring looked down at her. Next to her was Moira, poised to throw another rock down.

"Spring? Moira?" Gina looked back to her friends and saw they were still in the water beside her, one treading water, the other...

Gina turned her eyes back to the hole above them. She was in shock, that was what was up, somebody was fucking with them, and she was in shock, but that was no excuse to act stupid. She had to be practical.

"Look," Gina called. "I don't know who you fuckers are, but we've had enough of your bullshit. Throw us some rope! Call the cops! This isn't funny anymore." Gina paddled around, stretching her toes to find something solid to rest on. Nothing but warm water. She cocked her head up to petition their tormentors anew but choked when she saw another girl peek down the tunnel. It was herself; Gina waved down at Gina.

"Gina?" Moira whimpered.

"What?" Gina's sudden dizziness caused her to sink completely under, and she surfaced clumsily, trying not to throw up. "*What?!*"

"I think I know why Spring was so cold earlier."

"Oh the fuck you do. You better keep swimming, Moira! You hear me? Swim until help comes." Gina angrily splashed water onto Moira's face, but the other girl didn't even flinch, her eyes wide. She was clinging to Spring again, the drowned one, and her fingers were digging so deep into their friend's pale shoulder that black ooze was leeching out.

"You bitches!" Gina yelled up the cave. "Who the fuck are you?!"

Spring, the Spring in the world above, where the rain fell but would stop in an hour, leaving everything steaming in the summer sunshine, laughed, and her laughter echoed and bounced off the water, rattling through Gina's ears. The three girls disappeared, but Gina heard them singing Moira's version of "Dive." Gina, *the real Gina*, she told herself, joined in, trying to keep her shit together, but pretty soon she grew tired and just listened. The light was fading, or maybe the hole above them was receding, and Gina's weary limbs barely carried her over to where Moira clung to Spring's heavy, bobbing body.

"Dive! Dive! Dive! Dive with me!"

The singers grew distant, their song trailing away in the deepening dark, and then the cave went silent, save for the occasional splash and thrash from whatever was still alive within it. Up above, on the empty, desolate rim of the sink, the only sound was the pattering of rain on the surface of the water.

The Debt Collector

Fi Michell

In the spring of 1936, I arrived in Little Drumstan. I intended leaving as soon as my business was complete.

Bored of watching the locals, I examined the dimly lit black-and-white photograph of a deer-hunting scene that hung on the wall above my table in the Wolf's Head Tavern, the only decoration not scallop-shaped. Judging by the Art Deco style, this wing was newly built, doubtless thanks to the hamlet's thriving tourist trade. The din of the pounding rain mingled with laughter and singing.

Cold wind parted the smoke haze. In the open doorway, a man in an old-fashioned hooded greatcoat bent over his wooden cane. By my wristwatch, precisely nine p.m., as we'd agreed. I stubbed out my cigarette and signalled.

The hood concealed his inspection, but I felt it nonetheless. The same joint-weakening predator's scrutiny I'd learned to flee growing up in the Bryceter city slums. Not something I'd expected.

As he shuffled through the crowd, conversations paused. Several patrons nodded to him before returning to their beer. The proprietor signalled a waiter to take the coat, but the old man waved him away and leaned his cane against my table.

I stood, extending an open palm. "Mr. Devereaux, I am Marcus Slade. Thank you for coming. May I buy you a drink?"

"Mr. Slade." His voice rasped; his grip was icy and surprisingly firm. "No, you may not."

We sat, and he pushed back the hood, revealing a scalp as white as bone and sunken eyes set into bruises. If I'd not felt that gaze, he might still have been the elderly man I'd expected, so I looked for the spark deep within his pupils.

There it was. The faintest indigo flicker. My left hand clenched over old scars. A vampire, and only two feet of table between us. I kept my breathing steady. Did anyone realise? Vampires were despised and feared, unwelcome in decent places, and Little Drumstan had an enviable reputation for safety.

Well, I would not be deterred — he was, nonetheless, a legal entity. "You are aware I have purchased your debt."

"I read your letter," he said.

"Then you must understand I intend to collect it. Unlike my predecessors, I will not let things lie."

"Mr. Kermode and I had an arrangement with which we were more than happy."

"An arrangement in which you paid nothing, until the bank he worked for lost its patience. You are fortunate they sold your debt instead of chasing it through court."

Fear of what he'd do to them must have softened those before me, not pity for his age as I'd assumed. But I'd staked all my resources on this deal. His investments, leveraged against his estate, were lost in the crash of '29. They would never resurrect themselves. And it would be no use waiting for him to die.

"I'm not interested in informal arrangements," I said. "I need an offer with substance. I will repossess your estate if I must — though if I do, you will have nothing left. So I grant you one chance to sell your possessions yourself for a greater sum. I advise you not to waste the opportunity."

He smiled thinly. "Forgive me, Mr. Slade. I took the liberty of researching your company. Your business has only existed eight months, and you lack experience. This must be the reason for your haste, which, I advise *you*, is dangerous. It will not net the result you seek."

I mirrored his smile and leaned forwards. "Think what pleases you, but we shall come to an agreement. You have one week to detail your plan, then we will meet here again, and I will decide whether to accept it."

He sniffed. "Even if I do as you say, would it not be simpler to meet in your office? To discuss such things in a public bar lacks dignity."

"I have no office in Little Drumstan."

"Then perhaps we could meet at your accommodation? I dislike crowds. I am here tonight only for the sake of good will."

"I'm sorry, Mr. Devereaux. My address will remain private."

"Then may I invite you to my home? Unless you fear to see what you are costing an old man?" Despite the paperwork that proclaimed him eighty-three, he could have been far older, the quivering of his hunched shoulders restraining bestial strength and ferocity.

"Your sensibilities are not my concern. We will meet here this time next Friday. I will hear any proposition you have — I am not unreasonable."

He hissed at me like a cornered animal, and I froze. Long, bloodless fingers replaced his hood, then tightened around the brass knob of his cane. He rose without another word and shuffled to the door. Even after it closed behind him, cold lingered in my bones, and I drew from my pocket the token Leesa had given me before she left, a last keepsake. The ornate silver crucifix gleamed in the dim light. As I held it, the chill faded.

I'd not seen her in the past two years — except in my dreams. She would not look at me again until I became a greater man; someone of substance, with real wealth behind me. I could not blame her. Our spirits were the same, driven by the need to banish poverty with all its horrors. Though I'd proved myself in every other way, how could she trust me to keep her safe from that?

I had little time. Each passing day, she spiralled further into the realms of money and power. Far safer there than with my love alone. She had outgrown me, and my need for her was still great.

◆

The following week, I spent the days taking long walks, growing familiar with Little Drumstan. I bypassed the tourist shops, full of antiques, fine woollen garments, and mediocre artworks. Instead, I preferred to walk the high, stony ridge overlooking the moors.

Leesa would have loved the clean spring air that flowed up from the heather and stung my lungs, its cold bite compelling a surge of vitality. She would have loved the rolling hills and the ancient escarpments pushing their granite crags up through the mist. Most of all, glimpsed past the forest within its gates and commanding views of the moors, she would have loved Devereaux's brooding stone mansion set upon the village edge.

In the evenings, my nose and cheeks still smarting from the change to warm air, I sank into the leather lounge near the fire in Mrs. Appleby's guesthouse library, imbibing her house Scotch and reading her collection of local legends. The tidy streets beyond the curtains seemed benign; nothing so dangerous as those where Leesa and I learned the art of survival.

♦

I waited over an hour in the tavern on Friday evening, more than long enough to confirm Devereaux wouldn't show. Stubborn old monster. I wrapped my coat close, pushed on my hat, and set out into the night.

It was a short walk back to the guesthouse and long since I'd feared the dark. Yet my shoulder blades began to itch as I wound my way along the cobbled path, and, as I passed a row of old terrace houses, the hairs at the back of my neck bristled. An unmistakeable feeling. He was following me.

Cloud dimmed the moonlight, deepening the hollows between the buildings. The wind whispered in my ears, and I strained to hear beyond the echo of my footsteps. Dogs howled from one side of the neighbourhood to the other, like the wolves of old.

I drew the sharpened timber stake I'd hidden in my coat, though I'd no wish to fight a vampire on my own. Maintaining a steady pace, I took the shortcut across the green. Mist blanketed the central pond, spreading tendrils across the wet grass to finger empty park benches shrouded by weeping willows.

My sense of him watching never wavered, yet I reached the far side and crossed the road into the glow from the guesthouse windows unharmed. Perhaps he sought only to frighten me, to weaken my resolve. Entering, I nodded to Mrs. Appleby in the lounge and went straight upstairs to prepare for the night. I checked my window was locked, then draped the chain of Leesa's keepsake around my neck so the crucifix covered my heart.

Once in bed, I could not sleep.

Something scratched against the window, over and over. I'd booked the cheap room above the kitchen at the rear, and there were no trees near that wall. The crucifix grew warm. Pressing my pillow over my head, I tried to ignore the thin scraping only to drift into nightmares, fragments from my youth, reliving the twice that vampires had almost drained me dry. In the morning when I shaved, my eyes were bloodshot. The scars on my left hand and around my body throbbed.

I joined my fellow guests down in the breakfast room: an elderly couple who talked loudly about spotting turtle doves and blue tits, and a young couple on their honeymoon, giggling over boiled eggs and bacon. Above the lonely setting at my table lay a fine parchment envelope. An elegant hand had inscribed my name on the front.

"'Twas hand-delivered this morning," Mrs. Appleby said. She offered me stewed prunes, which I accepted, then hovered next to my shoulder as I turned the letter over. An untidy circle of red wax sealed it shut. I'd given Devereaux a post office box, but this had to be from him. He must want to be sure I knew he'd found me.

Sliding my knife under the seal, I eased the envelope open. "Mrs. Appleby, do you mind?"

She stepped back. "I'm sorry. It's just — it's unusual for anyone to receive a letter from the master."

"You mean Devereaux? Is he your master?" Her cheeks seemed far too ruddy for someone enthralled.

"Just tradition, sir, a way of thinking. We locals owe his family an enormous debt."

"Is that so?"

She poured me tea. "Oh yes. Many years ago, before his uncle arrived, there were a spate of deaths upon the moors. Several poor souls from this village were abducted, my own grandmama amongst them."

"I read about the old moors. I'm sorry. They must have been terrible times."

She set the teapot down. "Then you know about the packs of wolves that roamed there. Huge, shaggy beasts they were, and cunning, with eyes glowing as red as if the furnaces of hell were lit behind them."

"You saw them?"

"My poor mama did, when she were sixteen, from out her bedroom window. She said she couldn't breathe for the fear."

"I'll bet she couldn't."

"'Twas rumoured they'd been wicked men who sold their souls to the devil, then tried to undo their bargain." She pursed her lips. "Most city folk think them myth, or mere vicious animals, but they still run the moors in lesser numbers. Sometimes, they venture into other hamlets, but you won't read about that in the city papers. Anyhow, they never enter Little Drumstan, not any more. Sugar?"

"No thank you."

"My grandmama went out that night to see what frightened the hens. Later, she were found with her throat torn out and her chest eaten away." Mrs. Appleby stared into space, then took a deep breath. "Well" — she began spooning sugar lumps into my cup — "Mr. Devereaux's uncle arrived then. He'd married the lady, Cressida, the only child of the Langleys that owned the estate, after a whirlwind romance when she were staying with relatives in Bryceter. When they came home, they promised the deaths would stop, though bullets were as grains of rice against those beasts. No one ever knew how, but they did it."

Our local priest when I was growing up, the Reverend Haggart, had warned us powerful vampires held sway over wolves, but that was one thing I'd not had the chance to witness in the city. "Remarkable."

"They had no children of their own, but young Mr. Devereaux moved in after his uncle died and continued their work."

I sipped my too-sweet tea. "He is old. Does he still hunt?"

"He has no need. The wolves stay away."

She offered me a basket from which I selected a cinnamon roll.

"Little Drumstan is the perfect country destination these days," I said. "Your guesthouse must do well, especially being here on the green. The village is so pristine compared to most places — strolling back last night, I noticed no tramps sleeping on the park benches."

"Oh, Mr. Slade, we're not like the city. That kind of person doesn't come here, not since we closed the parish workhouse after the Great War. Perhaps they know they're not welcome. But as I was saying, those of us who've been here several generations — we remember what we owe. The master comes out rarely, but when he does, we look after him."

"He does seem reclusive. Still, he must visit for supplies."

"Henry, his manservant, keeps a vegetable garden and runs his errands when he needs something particular, like today."

She went off to ready my boiled eggs, while I perused the letter. And it seemed I had made an impression on Devereaux, for this was progress, although I disliked receiving a second invitation to his home.

However, I announced on her return, "Mrs. Appleby, I will dine with Mr. Devereaux at his estate tonight."

In fact, he'd made an offer I couldn't resist.

♦

The stake would be too long to conceal without my overcoat, so I strapped my two knives, each blessed by Reverend Haggart, beneath my shirt sleeves. A precaution, since I would never trust Devereaux's kind — but my nerves tingled with anticipation. The vampire had disclosed his mansion hid an undeclared art collection, including valuable works by masters. This evening I would survey them for myself. He had assured me I would discover something to my liking that would begin to address his debt — and he'd done his research again. I had one original painting on the wall of my city apartment — an excessive decoration, albeit small — a Eugène Guillaume. I'd never imagined owning such a thing, but I'd admired it so much I'd accepted it from my single earlier client to complete his payment.

I walked from my lodgings to the mansion that evening. The night was clear and, this time, did not seem so foreboding. The wrought iron gates waited open, and I crunched along the gravel driveway through the copse for several minutes before the mansion emerged in all its dark glory. Now I was here, it could not have felt more isolated. However, wall-mounted lanterns illuminated expansive entrance steps, and I strode up. The large brass door knocker was an odd whimsy in the shape of a wolf's paw. I gave it two solid raps.

Muffled footsteps, then the right door leaf swung wide, held by a short man in a tailored grey uniform — Henry. He bowed and waved me into a musty hall dominated by an enormous crystal chandelier and surrounded by a sweeping staircase. Devereaux descended with reverberating taps from the fine brass tip of his cane, the paper-thin skin over his cranium translucent in the reflections from a thousand crystal shards.

The paintings lining the hall could have been by some master, but were so decrepit as to be worthless. Their mildewed surfaces blended into the aged timber panelling, with hints of dull gold where light bounced off their frames. I bit my tongue restraining my disappointment.

Henry took my overcoat and ushered us into the dining room. I blinked — the lighting here suited a gallery, showing off well-preserved works. Immediately above the magnificent, though empty, central fireplace, a single piece demanded my attention: a portrait of a young woman from the last century, pink cheeked with cool blue eyes. Ringlets of dark red hair framed her face, and a fur draped her shoulders. I found the signature in the top right corner: *Bargeron.* Incredibly rare.

I dragged my gaze back to Devereaux. "She is very beautiful."

"That is Cressida. She died of a heart attack when bombers flew over during the war."

Devereaux and I sat at opposite ends of the long mahogany table, far from one another. That suited me, especially since my end was nearest the door. I wished I had my overcoat back, for the air was cold as a crypt, an association enhanced by the stone walls.

"The paintings here are very different to those in the foyer," I said. A quick appraisal told me the rest of the works were fine, but Cressida's portrait could be worth more than his mansion.

Devereaux nodded. "These ones have meaning for me — collecting each was a shared joy. It pains me to give up a single piece. Nonetheless." He shrugged. "I have you here."

Henry poured our wine from an elegant crystal carafe. I swirled the liquid and sniffed it, then rolled a drop upon my tongue — coppery. The liquid appeared cloudy when I held it to the candlelight. Devereaux quaffed his with obvious pleasure, and a rosy tinge infused his lips. If I was not mistaken, he'd tainted it with blood, from what creature I didn't want to know. Had he thought I wouldn't notice? Was this his idea of a joke?

Anger would only satisfy him. I focussed on the still life behind his head: a water jug and bowls of fruit in rich colours — possibly a Fleury? — as Henry served me pulled pork. It was cold, dulling the flavour. I chewed slowly, then not at all, letting the meat sit on my tongue as unwelcome memories flooded back. I couldn't be sure after so long that the meat was the same.

I set my cutlery down. "I've not eaten pork for many years. Not since my childhood."

"These days I always offer pork on the rare occasion I have guests." He had not touched his plate, as I'd expected. "It is Henry's specialty. But I hope you also enjoy the fresh vegetables from the garden. I pride myself on being self-sufficient." Glass in hand, he leaned back and arched an eyebrow. "And, where did you grow up?"

"With my grandmother, in poverty." I didn't want to name the place, not with that flavour in my mouth. That winter had been so cold, anyone on the streets died. Even the vampires who fed in the slums had left to sleep somewhere they wouldn't wake frozen. We had not eaten for several days when I helped Gran haul the body of a man who'd died on her doorstep down into the cellar. That night, and for a week to come, we ate well. *Waste not, want not*, she always said. She invited immediate neighbours and saved several children from starvation, including Leesa. And, it wasn't the last time. But when I scrounged through the pockets of the dead from then on, I saw my face in each of theirs, and feared one day I might not only die the same way, but be cannibalised.

"Let us discuss your offer," I said. "It is most attractive."

"We shall take a closer look at the collection after you've dined. And then — you can leave a poor old gentleman alone."

I had no intention of dining further. "That won't be necessary. I have already chosen the painting that will do."

"Yes?"

"Cressida" — and, the more I looked, the more it reminded me of Leesa. "Give me Cressida, and I shall disturb your peace no more."

The bruises beneath his eyes darkened, and the candles flickered. For an instant his face held a monstrous aspect, all his skin drawn taut, but it was reined back in a second. "You will choose another."

"Mr. Devereaux, give me Cressida, and I will be out of your life forever. Otherwise, you will lose everything."

"You do not understand what you ask." He stared at the table and set his wine down. His hand remained flat, pressed hard over the base of the glass. "Do you know the power of true love?"

The bitterness in his voice compelled me to meet his eyes at last. They deepened into black pools and anguish seeped into my mind, turning all colours grey. Each painting became a miserable parody.

How could I take his last memory? I should back down, be thankful with whatever he chose to give. My left hand cramped. I rubbed the scar and formed a fist around Leesa's token in my pocket. Its heat against my palm restored the fiery reds and oranges in the artworks, and in my own heart. "I know true love as well as any man might."

"It can transform one's very nature. Please reconsider. I cannot give you what you want."

A vampire claiming transformation? "Interesting theory." Well, I knew now Cressida had certainly been his wife. "But I don't believe true love requires the loved one to change."

"True love may change the one who gives it."

I pushed at my pork with my knife. Vampires could not change. "Surely any such change is only suppression. If the loved one is lost, the original nature will return."

His hands clenched, then he flattened them again. "Not if the memory is kept alive and honoured."

"But why should a reminder be needed if the transformation is real?"

His fingernails seemed to sharpen until their tips dented the table. "You have never known true love."

I stood. "Mr. Devereaux, none of this is relevant. Thank you for your… hospitality. You have forty-eight hours to get used to the idea of parting with the portrait. By Monday, I must receive it at my lodgings.

If not, you will face the loss of your magnificent estate. I imagine your current status is worth more to you than any painting."

He snarled and seized the end of the table so violently I was surprised it did not splinter. I left before I provoked him beyond control.

But he was not the only one in turmoil.

I'd seen enough to know he was powerful, and, from what he'd said, if I took his painting I would be unleashing a monster. If I took his estate, I expected the same result. So if I proceeded at all, if the legends were true, his protection of the village would cease, and the wolves would return.

Much as I wanted my fortune, I'd no wish to see innocents harmed. But there was also the matter of the pulled pork. It had been so long ago, I'd need a second opinion to be certain of its origin. As I walked home, my suspicion grew with each empty bench and doorway.

♦

Contacting Leesa for her opinion might only reopen old wounds. Besides, my business had yet to bear fruit. Over breakfast, I glanced through the social pages of the *Bryceter Sunday Times* seeking her image, which I often found there. She smiled out at me again, a bittersweet pleasure, for today she looked ecstatic, her slender neck sporting a glittering diamond necklace. That central stone looked the size of a quail's egg.

"Isn't she beautiful," Mrs. Appleby said from behind my shoulder, doubtless curious about last night. "Oh, she'll make a wonderful bride for Lord Walton."

I wrenched my gaze from the jewels and skimmed the article below. It took all my self-control to fold the paper neatly shut. I withdrew to my room in silence.

This could not happen. I'd had no time. Devereaux had talked of true love — had he ever had to deal with such an outrage?

I paced the floorboards. I could leave the village, and they'd continue to live in peace. I'd lose everything, but if Leesa married another, it no longer mattered.

Or did it?

If I was right, innocents were dying. Just how far did Devereaux's local "arrangements" go?

Mrs. Appleby would know, though she'd never admit it outright. She'd said there'd been no vagrants since the Great War — the time of Cressida's death. What if the local police turned a blind eye for the greater good? Perhaps the local bank manager refused to collect the debt for the sake of the village's protection. The homeless would be a convenient price to pay.

Leesa would need to come with me to his home. She would know if I'd imagined that flavour. But that would endanger her — especially cruel since her life had made a spectacular turn assuring her future. What right did I have to put her at risk?

And if I did nothing?

No one else would do anything.

Perhaps I just wanted to see her again; perhaps I was being greedy or selfish. I shut those thoughts out of my mind. A difficult letter to write, but I told her everything. I did not beg. She could decide for herself whether to come, if these things mattered to her — she might have changed in the last two years. Then, I wrote to Devereaux. I proposed inspecting the paintings again to consider a different arrangement, in order to wangle a second invitation to dinner.

♦

Two Saturdays later, I waited as the train chuffed into the station and hissed to a stop. I adjusted my hat and tie. My breath caught as Leesa stepped from the front carriage, smart in a loose, calf-length skirt and tailored jacket, her softly waved auburn hair reaching her shoulders. She'd come alone, as I'd asked.

Nearing her, I couldn't help myself. I bent to kiss her. Her lips met mine without hesitation, though briefly. We drew apart, and I offered to take her bag. She sighed.

"It's good to see you again, Marcus. I'm glad you understand how things have worked out. I've missed you, you know."

Torture. I smiled. "I do understand. Thank you for coming."

She did not reply, but her lips curved upwards, and she let me guide her to the taxicab arm in arm. We took in the local shops, which she enjoyed, then visited the high ridge along the moors, which she loved as much as I'd hoped.

Later, we dressed for the evening, a formal occasion. Her cream backless gown made me want to both stare and turn away in anguish. I could not forget her fiancé — she wore his necklace. I had to concede, with her hair swept up, it looked perfect.

And so together we graced the threshold of Devereaux's mansion. Henry welcomed us into the hall. Candles mounted in wall sconces combined with the central chandelier in a display that would have suited Christmas.

In the dining room, the central fireplace burned cheerfully, a basket of split firewood ready beside it. Devereaux stood tall behind his chair at the head of the table, in well-cut attire and absent the cane, which leaned by the hearth. With colour infusing his usual pallor, he looked, at most, fifty years. Our places were set at the same end as his to either side as though we were family.

He raised Leesa's hand to his lips. "An honour to meet the woman who has melted Marcus's heart." His voice had become smooth as velvet. "I have much for which to thank you — he has relented in the name of true love. Yet, I hear you are engaged to another."

Tonight, in the light of the candelabra, I could see how Cressida could have fallen for him. He was no filthy, ravaged creature like the vampires Leesa and I had once known. He kept hold of Leesa's fingers, and I admired her composure. She appeared neither discomforted nor enticed.

"A pleasure to meet you, Mr. Devereaux," she said. "And, yes, you hear correctly. Nonetheless, I wanted to see Marcus again. One last visit, while I still have my freedom."

He released her fingers. "Then let us begin. Henry?"

Henry drew Leesa's seat out. We sat, and he served — roast pork tonight. Cressida's likeness looked down on Leesa from above the fire.

Leesa tried a bite. I waited. Her face paled.

"I'm terribly sorry." She rose and backed away from the table, one hand over her mouth, blinking apologetically at Devereaux. "I'm afraid I feel ill."

A shadow visited Devereaux's features.

I placed my napkin beside my plate. "Excuse me." I rose and went to help her. "Shall I take you home?"

"Please." She linked her arm with mine. "You were right Marcus. This *is* just like old times."

We would leave at once, call in the Bryceter police, regardless of the consequences for the village. "I apologise," I said to Devereaux. "We must —"

"To leave without eating." He stood. "Twice in a row —"

"Leesa is ill."

"And I am not stupid. Henry — if you please."

I whirled around in time to see the doors closing. They clicked shut, and I heard a key turn in the lock. The candelabra dimmed; my senses heightened. I smelled Leesa's sudden sweat.

"So," Devereaux said, "there will be no more pretence."

Leesa backed towards the fire.

"You would both have left unharmed," he said, "had you eaten and were I convinced you would leave me alone." His gaze bored into me. "What I do not understand is why you had to bring the girl."

The cross beneath my shirt heated. I put myself between the two of them. The last illusion of haleness departed his body. His skin withered until I could not guess the age of the frame his suit hung upon: my knives were useless: the obscenity before us was older and far stronger than any we'd encountered in the slums. His focus switched past my shoulder to Leesa; he moved forward —

"You don't want to kill her," I said. "She is too like Cressida."

Depthless black pits shifted their attention to the portrait.

"You loved her," I said. And that moment, I knew it as truth, hard as it was to reconcile with the creature before me. "Before this, I did not believe a monster could feel."

He snarled. "And now? Do you think somehow because they look alike you may go free?"

I could hear Leesa's breathing behind me and sensed her effort to hold steady. Fighting wouldn't help; if he entered a frenzy we were both lost. My mind ransacked everything I knew of both him and myself.

"In the darkness," I said, "after Leesa left me, I thought I could not go on. But I found hope in the Creation that allowed her existence; in living things; the heather piercing the snow — I think of her as I walk the moors. And my pain magnified the meaning I found in art." His eyes narrowed upon me. "But you — though you say you shared Cressida's passion — have bought no new artworks since her death. You cannot, even after all these years. You are capable of emotion, but not of living or growth. What you have left is a mockery of life, a sham that would have broken Cressida's heart."

I had felt his misery under his gaze the other night; now, the room's shadows deepened and warmth drained from the air. I said, "I can help you end your agony."

"You would convince me to destroy myself?" He hissed, and his hands flexed, extending razor-sharp fingernails.

"I will take your ash and sprinkle it on Cressida's grave, on consecrated ground. You will be together."

"But you must believe that profane."

"Not when you truly loved her."

Wind gusted in the chimney. Behind me, in the hearth, a burning log snapped. Devereaux stared at Cressida's portrait again.

"I know about the wolves," I said. "She would not have wanted the homeless as the price. I bought your debt; I will own all you have upon your passing. I will put it to delivering the village in your stead."

"You? You do not have my power." His voice was harsh, and his gaze drank me in; the walls ceased to be: I was on the moor, wolves snarling all around.

My crucifix seared my chest; I dragged myself back. "I've learned to prevail," I said. "I have reason to live, but yours has gone. She left you twice cursed: neither human nor fully vampire: you cannot enjoy a vampire's first purpose, to feed, without betraying her. Yet keeping the village safe in her memory is not enough."

Shadows danced on the wall behind him. His face twisted in torment as the last remnant of the man he'd once been fought the darkness. His claws began to retract. For the first time, I began to believe a vampire might truly change. My heart pounded in my ears.

And I realised, as his gaze held mine, he, too, was listening to that.

"No," he said. "It is not enough."

His fingernails extended again. The indigo sparks in his pupils surfaced as the last of his humanity drowned. All I could hope was to hold his attention. With one swift motion, I yanked my collar loose; tilting my head to the side, I offered him my jugular.

His fangs elongated, then he was upon me, greeting me with all the dread agony from my nightmares. I screamed as he bit down into my neck; my muscles grew taut, and my fingers scrabbled, tearing at him. Blackness spread through my body; every scar ached with the new wound's intensity. His chest shuddered against me as the feeding ecstasy took hold; my cross sizzled between us, and I could smell my flesh burning. My limbs slackened in the dullness that followed. Through it all, I waited for her. I never could bear her to be the one to take this.

And a blow sent us crashing to the floor, the weight of the vampire on top of me. His jaws wrenched away from my neck; his agonised howl shredded my hearing. He arched backwards, clawing the air behind his head, but Leesa evaded him; with a split log, she hammered the cane further in. He spasmed; I shoved him off and rolled onto my hands and knees. As he lay writhing beside me, sparks traced the shrivelled surface of his skin, burning through his suit until he smouldered and flickered like the embers in the hearth. Cold wind filled the room, and he collapsed to ash. In its midst lay Devereaux's cane, charred up half its length.

All was still.

Leesa seized a napkin from the table. "Here" — she knelt by me — "I'll stop the bleeding."

As she pressed the cloth onto my wound, I hugged her, hard.

Vampires. They always assume she's harmless.

◆

When I was ready, we broke out of the room and overcame Henry. In the morning, we called the county police. They verified Devereaux's fate and took stock of everything, led by the stench to the pigpens around the back beside a large barbecue pit. They found three rotting straw beds inside the pens, one still occupied by a feral, wild-haired woman who cowered at the sight of Henry, though he was handcuffed. Punctures covered her emaciated body wherever her thin blanket did not.

Scarf wrapped around my neck, I checked out of the guesthouse.

Not long afterwards, I ran into Mrs. Appleby at the grocers. She stared at me, stony-eyed, and refused to return my greeting. Outside her guesthouse, vagabonds had begun to spend the night on the park benches. And upon the local moors, their protection removed, the first mutilated body had been found.

I had expected Leesa would return to the city. Instead, she sent her necklace back and stayed with me. Money had brought her societal demands, but not an escape from her memories — and, it turned out, she still loved me. The first thing we did after I claimed the estate was burn the pigpens to the ground.

Since then, I have been in consultation with the Reverend Haggart. Fortunately, I have always been drawn to hunting.

Every night, Leesa and I lie together, listening as the mansion walls collect the sounds of the moor. Outside our bedroom windows, the wolves' howls echo between the granite crags.

The Death Bell

Laura Ellen Joyce

Grainne could hear death again. The tops of her ears were pink and itchy, crusts of hard skin were beginning to form. She took the crochet hook out of her basket and worked them off in flakes, a swirl settling on the half-finished chair cover. It wouldn't matter, she'd wake up soon and her ears would be twice as bad, until, like when her grandmother had died, she'd hear nothing at all but the swish of blood, her ears gummed shut with pus and mucous. Now, all she could hear was a far off sweet tremble. Her great-uncle Jimmy had known what that meant, he had told her when she was four years old. That's the death bell my angel. I hear it too. The death bell, Grainne said out loud, knowing that this time it was for her.

Grainne was fifty years old. There'd not been much of a celebration when the half-century had hit. She was old-fashioned; even as a child, back home, she'd clung to her granny and sat in smoky rooms listening to half-understood gossip, whilst her cousins ran wild in the fields. Fifty suited her fine. Even in London, she had her local grocer, the Druckers, though it wasn't what it used to be at all, and Mass, always Mass. It had been a comfort to really settle into her spinsterish life. The women at work were always trying to get her to go out with them to happy hours and God knows what, even tried to send her on a blind date. One perky young madam had suggested they go clothes shopping. She had always been fond of her mother's good quality wardrobe, and she felt at home in the long black dresses and silk gloves. Seen by some young ones as affectations perhaps, but dignity had its cost. And besides, there was another reason she'd been happy to turn fifty. If the disease hadn't struck her by forty-five, it wouldn't get her at all. So she'd sailed on, blindly, making chair covers and bottling jam as though there was all the time in the world. And it was natural, she'd said to herself, that as she got older, she'd need less sleep. Natural to feel tired to her bones. She took brisk walks and made nourishing soups, took a spoon of cod liver oil every night and a stout every Sunday. But she'd been worried for some weeks now that she wasn't sleeping well at all. The pressure building up in her ears was the final truth.

Grainne took the basket with the chair cover and walked to her kitchen. She threw the whole lot in a black bag. She took out the first-aid kit from the high cupboard, thinking, who is it that I'm hiding it from? And removed two bottles from it. They'd both got the stamp of the hospital on them. She'd written them off as damaged on her shift yesterday. Taking two of each, dry swallowing them in succession, she replaced the bottles. She let an hour pass, watching the News 24 channel, and then, when the calm had taken hold, she sat at the telephone table in the hall and took out her small phone book, covered in patterns of roses and biro'd scribblings. She put a call through to her sister.

♦

It was Friday payday and everyone was in good spirits. Ryan and Sarah met for dinner. It was their third date. He wasn't really her sort, but she was sick of all the getting to know people, the abandoned plans, the way she caught herself looking over in restaurants, in bars, for someone better. Three dates was a good run, she'd stick it out. He was already there when she arrived, wearing an expensive-looking dark green jumper and holding a bunch of tulips. They were all different colours, bright and ugly. She rolled her eyes before she could stop herself, what was she supposed to do with them? But he looked good, smelled good when he stood to kiss her cheek. She tried to focus on that, until he pulled out her chair and she got the giggles. He'd be no fun to fuck, she thought, too chivalrous.

Sarah, you look fantastic. He pushed her chair in again, with her on it. Then he sat back down. She hadn't been to the restaurant before, it overlooked the river, there was a cocktail terrace on the roof. He looked very pleased with himself, as though he'd discovered it.

You look great Ryan. Nice jumper. She poured a glass of water into the blue tumbler already set out. She passed the carafe to Ryan. He smiled at her.

So, I hope you're hungry, he said. The candles heaped on their table were so bright; Sarah was glad she couldn't make out his grin too well in the glare.

Starving, she replied. He'd treated them to a taster menu, the least she could do was respond with enthusiasm. She sipped at her water and almost at once a waitress appeared asking if they were ready. Ryan said that they were.

This is good. Sarah said, genuinely impressed by the blood pudding; she loved the way that the black fat had cracked under the grill and oozed just a little. The delicate shards of bonemeal that gave it grit.

You're such a carnivore Sarah, Ryan teased, flirted maybe. She let him, it wasn't bad, this menu. He wasn't such a sap after all.

Save some room for dessert, the waitress, who was constantly at their table, said. It's a little bit special. She poured miniscule amounts of wine into their green tumblers, water into the blue ones. Sarah giggled. It was all so childish and pleasurable, she just let herself relax.

It really is special, the dessert. They put gold in it.

Gold? Sarah asked. It seemed ridiculous to her, such a city boy idea. Gold.

Doesn't it taste like shit though? She teased. His face changed. She continued. It's a great idea though, symbolic…

Sarah refilled both their wine glasses and when she placed the bottle back in the ice bucket, she brushed Ryan's hand with her fingertips.

♦

Grainne had been four when her grandmother had got the sickness. Four when she first heard the death bell. Adam, her nephew, was three now. Her sister, Mary, had been surprised to hear from her, but glad to have a few days peace whilst Adam visited Grainne; she'd sounded exhausted. Grainne had never met the boy before. She had not approved of Mary's defiant childbearing at forty-five. Her own phantom womb clenched, like a Venus flytrap, at the thought of it. The second time the death bell came, Grainne had been sixteen. There had been no baby in the end, just a slick of ruined tissue and a curdling violence inside her. She had had an operation to remove the cursed organs and she was glad; there was only herself and Mary now, and, of course, little Adam. Mary's man had been a sperm bank. Sperm. Bank. She spoke the words. Such an ugly thing it sounded.

The rain was coming down now, a horrid June, not a time for guests. But she'd made her plans, and she had such little time. She put on her good headscarf and took the big umbrella. She treated herself to a taxi to the airport. She'd be over and back in a few hours. Mary herself would be there briefly, and then gone. There was no mention of her coming over for a visit too. Grainne had a whiff of some man in the background, the eagerness she'd shown to get rid of the child, even for a few days. Well, that was to be expected from Mary.

She'd been to the shops and bought a few things for Adam's stay. And she had all the medicines he might need from the hospital, if he were sick. She was well prepared.

♦

Sarah and Ryan were walking along the river.

It was a nice idea Ryan, I just couldn't taste anything. But, really, it was a great evening. Forget about the gold.

Sarah was tipsy now; she just wanted to get to the next bar, to have another drink, it was Friday payday, summer had arrived. Ryan really was a bit wet after all. And maybe just a bit too flash.

You're right Sarah, forget it, everything else was perfect. He hadn't put his arms around her, she felt loose and warm, cushioned in the heavy haze over the river. The light was slipping away in pink slashes.

Whoops. Sarah slipped on something on the path; something slimy from the water. Ryan caught her for a second but she lost her footing and twisted away from him, before he could save her she was on her bum. The flat crack of impact sounded worse than the pain, but she'd be bruised later.

What the hell, why don't they clear up this stuff? She said. It's a fucking hazard.

What is it? Seaweed or something? It smells really bad. Ryan said. The pollution from the river was horrible, there was so much shit floating around in there. But he realised he'd been indiscreet, Sarah's face was white.

Sorry, I mean, it's not your fault, he continued.

What the fuck is that? Sarah said. What is it?

Ryan bent down and saw what she had slipped in. He turned away from her and vomited every course of the taster menu, right down to the gold.

♦

She wanted to do something nice for the boy. Have a little party for him. Give him some fun. Of course she'd like to take him for a blessing too, but she was too well known down at St. Francis's, and the father might not be too charitable under the circumstances. She had the candles and the holy water in the house anyway, there'd be no problem with that. She wondered if Mary'd even had him baptised. She'd left him in the parlour while she popped into work. There'd been an unavoidable meeting, some concern over lockdown procedures. And here she was again in the rain.

By the time she'd returned, Adam was sitting in the window seat watching the little girls across the road. He had flushed spots in his cheeks and looked happy. Good. He didn't turn around as she shook off her coat and put her bags down.

Adam, how are you darling? She asked him. He turned and smiled so wide she could see his two white teeth, and the chocolate she'd left him was smeared all over his face.

I want to play outside.

Now you know you can't do that you naughty boy, you're not well enough. She worried he would ask again and that would be a disaster. The two girls across the road were splashing in the dirty street, clapping their hands and shouting. Common.

Look what I brought you Adam, magic potion. If you have two swallows of magic potion your uncle and I will play a fun game with you, a game you never played before.

First I'll go outside then I'll drink the potion. Adam suggested. Smart smart smart. Smart as a whip and trouble. It broke her heart but he just couldn't go out.

Adam, remember what I told you about your lungs?

Lungs?

They are in your chest, look. She put her head to his chest and listened, with her mouth she made a heeeehaaaaw wheezing sound. Adam giggled. She tickled him under his armpits and he laughed louder and louder. Then he started to cough.

You see Adam, your lungs make you breathe and laugh and now they are poorly sick, you need to rest them and drink the magic potion to make them all better.

Then I can go and play with the girls? Tomorrow.

Tomorrow is your party. You will have better things to do than play tomorrow.

Adam's eyes were bright and she relaxed. She brought over the bottle of medicine with its plastic measuring spoon. She told him to lie still on the window seat for ten minutes then they would play a game. She put the rest of the stuff from the hospital in the high cupboard in the kitchen.

Where's my special boy? Where's my big, strong Adam? She picked him up and growled. Mmm I eat tasty little boys like you, yum yum yum. She pretended to bite at Adam's face, nuzzling him and finally giving him a big kiss on the forehead.

Again, again. Adam laughed and his aunt took the game out of the cupboard that she had bought for him before he arrived.

You spread out the sheet like this, she said, and you spin the wheel. Wherever the arrow falls, that's where you put your feet. Red, blue, yellow, green. I'll go first. Left hand blue.

As she bent down, her skirts fanning out behind her, balanced on one hand, Adam ran towards her, smacking her on the bum and running away again. For a minute he looked worried, sneaking behind the sofa, until Grainne began to giggle, and, pleased with himself, he started to dance on the spot, lifting his tiny fists in the air.

♦

Grainne had been allowed in with her grandmother at first. The two months where she was more or less lucid. She didn't sleep at all those months, just went into a viscous daydream from the medication. It was okay, because she still knew Grainne, still stroked her hair and let Grainne feed her chocolates that she bought with her own pocket money. There'd been enough talk between the women of what this disease meant, that Grainne had some idea, young as she was. The first two months are not so bad, no sleep at all, but as long as the body rested, it was possible to get some peace. Some of this was what she knew then, most of it, what she'd learned since, of course. It was all mixed up now. Then, the pain began. Four months without sleep and the skin became baggy, eyes red, heart faltered and crashed, speeding out of control to feed the weakening blood vessels. After one year with no sleep, a person died, hallucinating, screaming, thrashing. And there was no cure but death. Grainne had known all this somehow, the death bell had told her, and her great-uncle Jimmy knew it too. He was dead of course, they all were, her mother too, not of the disease though. If you'd not got it by forty-five you were alright. Grainne went in at the end, when no one was looking, and she spoke to her granny directly. Granny, I want to know if there's anything we can do, I don't want you to die, I don't want it. And granny had told her what to do.

♦

Grainne sat on the garage floor. She was tired, so tired, but there was much more to do. She went to the kitchen, rinsed her hair and hands in the old sink and stepped out of her clothes. She balled them into a black bag and washed more thoroughly, especially her hands and feet. She put on a paper gown from her nursing supplies. When it was done, she walked into the room that had been Adam's. The game of Twister was in there, some colouring books, a stuffed pig. The medicine was on the bedside table. Drowsy it said, not for under 12s. But it had been right to give it to him. She drank the rest of the bottle, two thirds almost. She lay down in the paper gown, on Adam's bed. Drowsy was how she felt.

◆

The body had been in the water for three weeks. It was coming apart. The cloths that had been wound around it were loose, it was them, green with algae, that Sarah had slipped on. Beneath the cloths, the body bulged. There was a bright orange shirt on the body, though this was falling apart too. No head. No limbs.

◆

Sarah was crying. Ryan was crying. They had been asked to move away from the area once the police arrived. Sarah put her arms around Ryan and he hugged her. They stood, looking down the river, blue lights and noise and helicopters spinning into nothing behind them.

What a terrible date. Sarah said. She laughed.

Ryan laughed too. Then he stopped, blushed. It had been a terrible date. And they could probably never go on another one.

It was a pretentious restaurant and I'm sorry I brought you there, he said. As though that was the problem. Sarah laughed. She laughed and laughed. She let go of Ryan and leaned against the railings. Ryan's hand hovered in the air, not sure whether to touch her shoulder again.

Want to come back to mine? She asked through broken giggles.

Yes, was all Ryan said.

◆

Peekaboo. Peekaboo.

Is it my party? Adam asked, sleepy now, from the medicine. He had his new clothes on, the orange shorts and shirt.

Yes my precious boy, it's your party.

Adam lay down on his side, his little fists curling across his chest.

I feel funny. He said. Like I'm dreamsing.

A tinkling sounded in the room. His aunt lay her hair across his face, and the smell of roses drifted into his dreams.

A Meeting in the Devil's House

Richard Dansky

No roads led to the house where I was going, and you couldn't find it on any map. Built before the War of Northern Aggression, it had wrapped itself in fog and moss and vanished into history like a leading lady walking offstage before the wrinkles could begin to show. To find it, you had to know where it was, and, to know where it was, you had to have been there already. This kept the fools and the drifters and the tax men far from her doors, allowing her to slowly crumble, at her own pace and without any witnesses.

But I had business there, and I knew where I was going. Had been there before, on business other than mine, and so the path was familiar. Officially the place was in Mississippi, or it had been once upon a time, but when I turned onto the dirt road that led down into the mist, all the names and labels went away.

The last time the house had been painted, it had been painted white. It still held that color in most places, the ones where vines hadn't wrapped themselves around columns and up waterspouts and given the place an accent in dark green. All those columns still stood, holding up the roof over a porch that by rights should have moldered into sagging, broken wood.

It hadn't. Nor had the front door fallen from its hinges, though the brass knocker that once adorned the heavy wood had long since been ripped out and carried away. I'd heard what had happened to the man who'd done that, once, and I had no need to hear that story ever again.

The door was unlocked, as I'd known it would be. I swung it open, and the floorboards sang under my feet as I stepped inside. Light punched its way in through clouds and cobwebbed windows, enough to see by but not enough to see well, but I already knew what I'd find. Old furniture under tattered drop cloths, stacks of old wood by fireplaces that would prove clean enough to use, and everywhere dust, dust, dust. Broad stairs still ran up to the second floor, with no holes or rotted-out boards that I could see. Then again, I couldn't see too far. Halfway up, they vanished into the dark.

I thought about going up there, just to see what was still there to be seen. Then I came to my senses, and went back to the kitchen. Sturdy furniture was all through the house, couches and beds and overstuffed chairs, but I'd be damned if I was going to sleep on it. I knew who owned this house, and the price he extracted for favors. Instead, I made a supper of what I had in my pack, then found a place against a wall to set myself for the night. I did set a small fire, more for light than for heat, but that was the only concession to comfort I made. And night fell, and the shadows wrapped their loving arms around the house, and the crackle of the fireplace mostly drowned out the ghosts in the hall.

♦

The next morning, the stranger came up the walk. He was middle-aged, finely dressed and going bald, and he had the guilty look of a man who'd lied to his wife about where he was going. Navy suit and nice shoes, now scuffed and muddy, and the watch on his wrist was heavy and expensive looking.

He stopped, maybe twenty feet short of the front steps, and pulled a handkerchief out of his breast pocket to dab at his brow. It was hot out, a sick, sticky heat that wrapped you up and held you a little too close, and, if the sun wasn't shining through the clouds, it didn't skimp on warming them. Water dripped off the trees, running down the beards of moss and tap-tap-tapping onto the wet ground while the stranger stood there and looked the place up and down. It was clear he wanted no part of walking forward; just as clear he couldn't go back.

He wiped his forehead again, then tucked the wet kerchief back in his pocket and took out a phone. I could have told him it wasn't going to work — nothing like that worked in that house, where time had kicked back and taken it easy a hundred fifty years prior. But I didn't say anything; some things a man has to figure out for himself.

I watched him try a few calls, get nothing, panic, and try again. About the forth go-round, when it looked like he might actually do himself some harm, I stepped out and called to him.

"Hey there," I said. "You looking for someone?"

He screamed, a little boy's scream that should have been funny coming out of a big man but wasn't. The phone fell down into the mud, and he started up at me with wide eyes.

"You… you…" he said, even as he knelt down to rummage for his phone. "You're… you must be… I'm here to…"

I held up a hand to stop his rambling. "Peace, friend. I've got no call to hurt you."

His jaw worked for a bit before words came back out. "You… is this your place?"

I shook my head. "Not hardly, though I know the owner. Supposed to meet him here, or at least that's what he asked me to do."

"Ah." The man sagged, like he was being held up by invisible strings just gone slack. "I'm here to meet someone, too. A business meeting." He looked around nervously. "I didn't know there'd be someone else here."

"He didn't tell me you'd be coming, neither," I said, and stepped down off the porch. He didn't move, didn't do anything but blink. I held out my hand to him. "Name's Eli."

He reached out for my hand, remembered he still had his phone, swapped hands, then realized he had mud on his fingers from the phone still. That led to a round of wiping his hands on his slacks, until he realized that they were expensive, which led to more fumbling, until I finally couldn't take any more, and took his hand for a shake.

"Olsen, Tim Olsen," he said. "I work in, well, never mind what I work in." He looked around then, straightened up, and cocked his head at me. "You set up inside?"

"I am," I allowed.

"Then what do you say we go in and talk. I don't like the look of that sky."

It wasn't the sky that I didn't like, but I wasn't going to tell him that. It was the sudden silence that had fallen down over the house and grounds. Somewhere, a drop of water fell off a tree branch and headed for the ground; the snare drum tat-tat it made when it hit was louder than it had any right to be. Otherwise, there was nothing.

Well, not exactly nothing. No sound, sure. But if you breathed deep and were looking for it, you'd find a faint hint of sulfur.

♦

I shut the door behind us when we walked in, but didn't lock it. Anything that was supposed to be here, it wouldn't do no good, and anything that was unwanted here set foot on the grounds to their own peril. Olsen let me lead him back to the kitchen, his head on a swivel as he took the place in.

"Nice," he said. "Must be expensive keeping this place up."

"I believe the owner has made certain arrangements," I replied, and kept walking. Behind me, I could hear Olsen choke for a moment.

The fire was low in the kitchen, so I built it back up while Olsen wandered around and poked his nose into the cabinets. "No food, I see."

"Nope," I replied. "But you're welcome to share what's mine."

"Thank you," he said, and nodded gravely. "I didn't realize I was going to need to accommodate myself, or I would have brought provision with. When I was told to come to this house…" He spread his arms wide and let his voice drop off. "You get invited to a man's house, you expect he's going to put food on the table."

"This is a special house," I said, keeping my voice neutral, and set about making some coffee. "Just as well not to eat or drink anything of this place. Don't want to find yourself obligated."

"Oh, I'm already —" he started, but a sound outside cut him off.

It was a howl, a long, high howl that climbed in through the windows and bounced itself off the walls. It was an angry howl, a hungry howl, and it was loud.

Which meant the thing that made it was close.

"What the hell was that?" Olsen asked, his face pale.

"Not sure," I said, though I was surer than most might have been. "Nothing you want to meet face to face, though."

Olsen nodded. "The windows shut on this place? Doors locked?"

I didn't have the heart to tell him that if it wanted in, it was getting in, so I just nodded.

"Good," he said, and shuddered as the howl came again. "Would hate to miss my meeting 'cause I got eaten."

"I don't think there's any fear of that," I told him, and pulled a couple of cups out of my pack. "Coffee's ready, if you want."

"Don't mind if I do." He walked over, throwing a glance down the hall as he did. The hand that took the coffee wasn't shaking, but there was tension in the fingers. Olsen himself looked like a bundle of tangled wire now, all jangled nerves stretched taut against one another.

"What kind of meeting are you here for?" I asked, and in that moment he dropped the cup. It was tin, so it didn't break when it hit, but the coffee splashed all around as it bounced and spun and rolled away.

We both watched it go, silent till it rolled to a stop in a corner. "Sorry," Olsen said. "Just… nervous about the meeting, that's all."

"I don't blame you." I nodded to the cup where it sat. "Refill?"

"If you don't mind."

"I don't mind at all."

♦

The day rolled on, and we drank more coffee, and talked about things that didn't matter at all. Olsen admitted he didn't quite know when this meeting of his was likely to be, since his watch had stopped working along with his phone as soon as he'd set foot on the property.

The howls stopped after the second one, at least until the sun went down behind those moss-hung trees. Thereafter we could hear them, faint and off in the distance, along with the sound of something big crashing through the trees.

They didn't get any closer, but, by the way Olsen kept looking at the door, I knew the man didn't want to sleep downstairs. Sure enough, he asked if there were fireplaces in the bedrooms upstairs.

"Might've asked that when there was still light," I said, but it was easy enough to rig a torch, and Olsen himself took an armload of wood from one of those neat piles. Then it was up the stairs and into the dark, with dust choking our footsteps and rising up to fill our lungs.

"Footsteps," Olsen said, coughing and pointing.

"Mine," I told him, and it was true. He waited for me to say more, and when I didn't, he kept moving. The hallway was broad, too broad for the torch to light properly, but what could be seen mirrored the downstairs. Cloth covered mirrors and art; dust covered the rugs and everything else.

"To the left," I told Olsen. "There's a bedroom at the front of the house. Or there was, last time I was here."

"You think the owner's changed things?"

"Not hardly."

And sure enough, there the bedroom was, its four-poster clean and uncovered, and its fireplace neat and ready for use.

Olsen stopped for a moment, so I busied myself starting the fire. After a minute, we had warmth and a fair bit of light, and he looked around the room.

There were no drop cloths on the furniture here. No covers on the mirrors, no hangings covering the portraits of men and women who'd lived and died in this house decades before. The dust stopped at the door, not a speck of it to be found.

"This isn't right," Olsen said. "This place was prepared."

"He knew you were coming, I believe," I said mildly.

Olsen shook his head. "But the dust outside. The footprints. This isn't right."

"Nothing here's right," I told him. "But here's clearly the place you were meant to be tonight."

"Oh." He looked surprised again. "In here."

I nodded. "But I reckon I'll stay too. No sense getting too spread out in a place like this. Too big for two men."

He blushed a little bit. "But there's one bed, and I —"

I cut him off. "I'll sleep against the wall. That bed's meant for you." Last comfort you'll have, I thought to myself, but didn't say. "Besides, I don't like owing a thing to the one who owns this place. Use of a bed for a night's more of a debt than I care to incur."

His mouth formed an *o*. "If you think I shouldn't —" he started.

"It's for you," I said wearily. "Trust me. Now get some sleep. You've been traveling. I'll keep watch, keep an eye out for the ghosts."

"Ghosts?" He thought about it for a minute, then came to a conclusion. "All right then. If a place on God's green Earth were to have ghosts, this surely would be it."

"They'll mostly stay in the hall," I told him. "I'll see to it. You get some sleep."

He sat down on the bed and shucked off his shoes. "Seems strange to be trusting a man I don't know to watch over me while I sleep in this place," he said.

I didn't turn my head away from the hallways, where the shadows were starting to move. "You're here for a reason that's stranger."

"How much do you know?" he asked. "About why I'm here."

"Enough. And you know I'm not here to do you harm."

"Not if you're here for the same thing I am." He snorted, then slid himself under the covers. "Night, Eli. Thank you for the watching."

"It's what I do," I told him, but he was already asleep.

◆

Morning came wrapped in fog, with no sign of our host. I portioned out breakfast from what was in my pack, coffee and some hard cheese and bread, and Olsen and I ate in silence. When we finished, I suggested we take a walk through the trees, as staying cooped up in the house was liable to make both of us a bit tetched. Olsen declined, however, saying whatever made those howls might still be out there. If I didn't mind, he'd stay in the house.

"You do that," I said, and took myself downstairs. All the dust was swept away now, I could see, and all the drop cloths had been pulled away. The house looked ready for company, though I'd neither seen nor heard anyone else during the night. 'Cept the ghosts, of course, but they had their own business to be about, and didn't seem the type to do tidying.

The front door was open, which didn't surprise me, so I walked down and out and into the trees. The fog was thick, rolling up to the edge of the porch and no further, but a dozen yards from the house it had vanished entire into the mist. Another man might have worried about getting lost; I just wanted to stretch my legs among the cypresses.

And as I walked, I saw him there. The owner, the one whose will kept this place as it was and ruled all within it.

The Devil.

He stood in the shadow of one of the trees, back pressed up against it, slouch hat low over his eyes. And he saw me, and he saw that I saw him, and he smiled for an instant before he vanished.

I knew better than to run over to where he'd been. There'd be nothing there; there never was. Instead, I kept walking, and there he was again, up ahead on the left. A nod, a smile, and he was gone again, only to reappear high up on a branch, then off in the distance, then behind me so close I could feel the heat of his breath.

"What do you want?" I finally said, with no hope of an answer.

"The last thing you think," he said, and then, with brimstone stink, he wasn't there anymore. I turned to look for him, knowing I'd find nothing but feeling like I ought to do so anyway. Sure enough, he was gone. Maybe there was a streak of reddish-black in the fog where he'd been, maybe there wasn't. But I was alone out in the fog, a long way from the house, and he knew where I was.

Off in the distance, and in the dark, something growled. Something big.

Maybe I wasn't as alone as I thought.

I ran. I ran for where I thought the house was, and I ran without looking behind me. The beast in the cypresses was on the move, I could hear that much, and it was coming my way. If I stopped, if I looked back, it would surely catch me, and then no power on Earth could save me.

So I ran, with branches breaking behind me, and, when the house loomed up out of the mist, I made straight for it. Up the porch and slamming the door behind me I went, pelting up those stairs.

"Eli?" Olsen's voice came from the room where I'd left him. I didn't waste the time to answer. Instead, I ran down the hall and in, and looked out the window.

After a moment, Olsen joined me.

"There," I said, and pointed down.

He looked. And he saw.

"What's that?" Olsen breathed.

"The owner? That's his dog," I said. Outside, a huge black hound scratched at the dirt with those claws the color of dried blood and old fires. Each paw was maybe nine inches across; each claw a good curved two inches. Its eyes were red, too, and too big for that wicked hound dog face they were set into. It stood there, steaming quietly in the rain while little tongues of flame licked in and out of its mouth like it was breathing. It took a couple of steps forward, and the turf where it had been standing was pushed down and burned black.

"It's huge," Olsen said after a moment's staring.

I shrugged. "The Devil likes big dogs."

"I'll bet he does."

The hound was sniffing the air now, muzzle raised and eyes narrowed.

"What's it looking for?" Olsen asked.

I thought about saying "us," but that'd be unkind. "You," I told him instead. "I'd hold still, myself. Make a noise, it's liable to hear you."

Olsen nodded, not trusting himself to speak. Instead, he backed slowly away from the window, one slow step after the other.

The hound was moving now, taking a couple of steps toward the house, then stopping to sniff the air again. I stayed where I was, watching it trot closer to the front door. Behind me, Olsen crouched down, shaking with fear. Both hands were over his mouth, the better to keep himself from making a sound.

◆

It stopped.

Looked up.

Those dried blood-red eyes met mine.

And then something made a noise off in the trees, and it was gone.

♦

"Mother of God," Olsen said, and collapsed onto the floor.

"I wouldn't say that," I told him, and offered him a hand up. He ignored it and sat there, rocking back and forth.

"I didn't believe," he said. "I mean, I knew, but I didn't believe. Oh, God, it's real, it's real, it's all real."

"That's why you're here, isn't it?" I pulled a bottle out of my pack, then sat down beside him. "You made the deal, your time ran out, and you came here to pay the piper."

Olsen nodded, miserable. "First I saw you, I thought you were him. Didn't realize you'd made a deal, too."

"My deal's different," I said. My deal was no deal, not worth explaining to a man whose last hours were running out. "But I was told to be here. Now tell me what happened."

With a shake, he pulled himself together. Behind us, the fire crackled and popped.

"I made a bargain," Olsen said. "Made a pretty good one, too. So I told myself, and, for a while, I listened."

"No deal with the Devil's a good one," I told him, and passed him the bottle. He took it, took a swig without pausing, and passed it back to me.

"I had an out, you see," he said, and wiped his mouth with the back of his sleeve. "You don't get those often, I don't think. But he gave me one."

I set the bottle down. "Damn near never," I agreed. "So what'd he give you?"

"The usual." Olsen shrugged. "Success, mostly. Success in everything I set my hand to. Business? Every venture was golden. Love? The woman I dreamed of fell into my arms. All of it, boilerplate and there for the taking."

I didn't say anything. It wasn't my place to do so.

"And he gave me a way out. Easiest one in the world." Absently, he reached for the bottle, and I slid it closer to him. "All I had to do was get someone to take the same deal I'd taken. Same benefits, same out clause, same everything. Do that, and the lien on my soul would be free and clear." He took another sip. "That was the plan, you know. Make my pile, then pass it along before the bill came due."

"What happened?" I prompted him. "Couldn't find anyone to take the deal?"

Olsen shook his head. The shadows were longer now, creeping across the floor like a flood of black water lapping up against us. "Found too many. Greedy men, desperate men, fools — all kinds. But I realized something."

"Sending another man to hell puts a mark on a man," I said without judgment. "I can see why you'd walk away."

Olsen wagged a finger at me, a schoolteacher's gesture for a student who jumped to the easy conclusion. "Not it at all. There's plenty of men that deserve hell that I've known, and most of them would have jumped at the chance for half of what I had. No, it was something else. I looked around, you see."

"Looked around?"

"Looked around. At the success that the bargain gave me. And I realized, it didn't just happen. It had to come from somewhere. If my venture prospered, it was because a dozen hardworking men saw theirs fail. Didn't matter if they were better or smarter or more deserving. If I set my mind to something, I'd have their success, and they'd be left behind."

He took a long pull on the bottle, then set it ruefully aside. "Same thing with my wife. She'd been with a man, a good man, when I set my cap for her. And he died, and she needed comfort, and God Almighty, isn't that still a canker in my soul."

He looked up at me then, and I met his eyes. He didn't look away, not for a long minute. "You see why I didn't pass it along, then?"

I nodded. "Another man takes that bargain, might not care about the damage he did along the way. Might enjoy it, even."

Olsen's face was grim. "Yep. And that, I didn't want to carry with me, 'cause it would be a hell all its own. Better to pay the bill on my own damnation than forge another link on that chain."

I thought for a moment, then chose my words carefully. "Sounds like you outsmarted the Devil, at least a little bit. He ain't going to like that."

"He set the terms."

"Doesn't mean he'll be happy when he figures it out."

"Look," Olsen said. "For twenty-five years, I've known I was going to hell. I've been waiting for this day half my life. Now the bill's come due, and I'm ready to pay. Ready to stop worrying, ready to stop living in fear. And this is the one thing I can take with me into the dark and into the fire — that I didn't drag anyone else down with me."

I thought about saying something, but something else beat me to it. There was a splintering crash from downstairs, the sound of old wood reaching its breaking point in a moment of sudden fury.

"What the hell is that?" Olsen shouted, and then there was a howl and another crash, and we both knew.

"He sent the hound for you!" I said, and rose up. "Quick!"

Olsen was up now, too, pale and sweating but resolute. "You think we can run from that?"

"I think we'd better!"

There was another almighty crack, and the sound of heavy wood hitting the floor. I grabbed Olsen by the wrist and ran.

At the top of the stairs, I looked down. The door was half gone, huge chunks of it gouged out and scattered on the floor. Through the gaps I could see the hound, its claws working at the remaining barrier in a fury.

"Before it sees us!" I shouted, and pulled Olsen along. He didn't resist, but he didn't help none, either. Instead, he just stumbled on, looking back toward the sound of claws scrabbling on wood.

"Why are you doing this?" he shouted. "Leave me!"

"Something's not right!" I ran down the hall, headed for the back stairs. Around one corner and then another we went, even as the thwack of wood on wood told us the hound had finished its work down below. "I saw him this morning. I talked to him, and he said —"

But then a howl rushed up from below and near bowled us over. I could hear claws on wood and the heavy thump of a body moving up the stairs; the hound was inside.

"There!" I said, and pointed to the back stairs. They were narrow, and they curved in a thin spiral too tight to take fast.

Too thin for the hound, too, I was thinking, and I shoved Olsen forward. "Down! Go!"

"What about you?"

"I'll be right behind you. Run!"

Run he did, even as a thud at the top of the stairs told me the hound had reached the second floor.

I thought about running and following Olsen. Thought about drawing the hound off and leading it on a merry chase through the house, hoping I still had enough of the Devil's favor that I might maybe survive. Thought about fighting, though I knew that was hopeless.

Behind me, Olsen's steps rang out loud against the wrought iron of the staircase. He was running for all he was worth, panting loud and hard as he ran. Ahead of me, the hound slammed into a wall at speed as it tried to take a corner. It shook its head, chuffed deep in its throat, and turned to work up more speed.

It saw me then, saw me standing there between it and its prey. Its ears went back and it growled, deep and low enough to shake a man's bones clear out of his skin. Flames twined up from its eyes, and from the corner of its mouth. Those claws, those big red claws, they dug trenches into the floor with every step as it advanced.

It occurred to me that I didn't know Olsen very well. It also occurred to me that I was doing a damnfool thing, and that I was about to do another.

Olsen ran. The hound advanced. And I held up one hand and said, "Sit!"

It sat. And it looked at me. And it laughed.

It laughed in the Devil's voice, of course. It laughed long and it laughed loud, and, when it was done laughing, it said, "Eli, I've got a special place for fools just like you. That was the bravest damnfool thing I've seen in a thousand years."

"Best be paying more attention," I said, and cocked my head. "You going to catch him and take his soul?"

"That was the bargain." The great red tongue was hanging out now, the hound panting with the effort of making human words. "I do keep my bargains."

"Bullshit," I said. "You keep 'em as far as you want to, and if you wanted his soul you would have taken it last night, proper and legal."

The hellhound nodded. "True enough. But he didn't keep his end of things."

"What the hell does that mean?" Down below, I could hear a door slam. Brave face or not, Olsen was running, and running like he meant it.

"Come on, Eli, half the fun for me's in the waiting. A man who's counting down to the day he's got to give up his soul, he counts down to the second. He knows how long he's got, and that's what he thinks on. Drives him crazy, it does. Makes him miserable. Spreads the poison of his impending damnation all around him, which makes it good business for me."

"But Olsen didn't panic," I said.

"He was ready to go," the hound agreed. "Least he was, until he met you. Till you came running into the house. Till you listened to his story and tried to save him when the big bad doggie came clawing at the door. Now, though, now maybe he's a little less resolved. Wants to live a little more, since someone put escape into his mind."

"You used me," I said.

"That I did, 'cause that's what you're for. And now you're going to stand aside, and I'm going down those stairs so I can run Mister Olsen clear back to daylight. And he can live the rest of his natural born life wondering every moment when he's going to see me again. Wondering when it's going to end, all sudden like. And wondering, just a little bit, if maybe he did get away after all." The hound looked at me, and suddenly it wasn't a hound, it was a wolf, and it was grinning that mean-wolf grin that means you're next. "He got some hope, and now that hope's gonna burn him every day for fifty years. Good work, Eli. Couldn't have done it without you."

With that he sprang past me, flowing down those steps with a rattle and a clatter and a howl. Somewhere, I could hear Olsen running, the beast nipping at his heels. I imagined him pelting through the trees, always one step ahead, never knowing he's supposed to be, until he stumbles out onto the road and hitches a ride, and tries to go piece his life back together. But a little hope in the mix, well, that was going to be a terrible thing, 'cause now he had something to lose.

If he ever saw me again, I'm sure he'd thank me. Thank me for saving him, thank me for stalling the hound long enough for him to get away. But he ought not to, not after what I did, and deep down, he'd know it.

I sank down to the floor and waited there a while, till the sun was gone and the ghosts were out, and the entire place just had its normal contingent of spirits. Then I picked myself up and made ready to go. Got my pack, doused the fire, and went on out.

And the front door, whole again and sturdy, shut itself behind me.

No Substitute

Steve Dempsey

At the other end of the table, my grandfather Buchan sits in his chair, the only one with the arms. Stiff collar, stiff back, stiff moustache. The servant stands over and beside him, a plate in his hand. He places the dish on the table and with the other hand withdraws the silver cover. There are two cubes of meat on the plate. The flesh is uncooked and speckled with bristles. My grandfather looks down. His expression has not changed. He picks up his fork, spears the cube on the right, and puts it in his mouth. He chews, for quite some time, and then swallows the morsel with neither pleasure nor distaste. He repeats these actions with the other cube. The servant reappears and removes the plate. My grandfather looks at me.

"Now, Stephen, your turn."

The servant places a dish in front of me and removes the cover. There are two cubes of meat on it. One is a darker shade than the other.

♦

"Lower away, faster! Or you'll ne'er see Nantucket again!" The master screams, his voice lost in the shrieking of the wind and onslaught of the waves. A cataract hits the *Barabarita* astern, raising the bow right out of the water, like an orca jumping. Men are flung about like droplets of icy water. The master, strapped to the wheel, is hit full in the face by the haft of a harpoon, the blood, the top of his head, lost in the ocean which has risen up to take them. In barely three minutes, the tip of the bowsprit is the last of the ship to be sucked under the chill waters.

◆

"What the hell?" Buchan struggles awake. He is restrained, wrapped tightly with strips of leather and animal skins, his arms pinned to his sides. He hears the soft pad and crunch of shoes on snow. Trees crowd in quietly and glide past him on either side, bending to inspect him, their laden branches springing and gently scattering flakes across the hide travois in which Buchan can now see he is being transported.

"Where?" says Buchan, not yet capable of forming cogent thought beyond the immediate concerns. The travois draws to a halt, and dark-skinned faces peer at him from out of layers of fur. And there, one white face under a raccoon hat. It's Ernst, one of the whaleboat oarsmen. He reaches out to Buchan, the sleeves of a native jacket halfway down his rough hands, tufts of grey fur thick with frost.

"Yur safe now, man. Safe and warm. These darkies pulled us out o' the surf. It's just me and you now. The *Barabarita* has gone, and your leg is broke." There is the bark of a dog, then many. A native says a sharp word, and the travois starts off again.

◆

Buchan stands outside the hut. His leg is held at an angle, set now, but he'll never serve on a whaler again. Winter has come round again, and early too. Ernst and he are still here in the native village. After the blooms of summer, the greens, yellows, blues, and reds, there are only two colours now, the white of snow and the black of night and forest. The men have a hut to themselves, built by Ernst whilst Buchan sweated with fever and pain, often strapped to a wooden frame to stop him from hurting himself. Ernst has been busy with more than just sapling, bark, and furs. From inside the hut, the *weetu* as he calls it, come the low tones of the chanting women. This has the rhythm of the ocean, of the oar, the in and out. Buchan thinks of his first time to sea, his soft hands rubbed raw against the grip, the sting and smell of the cod liver oil, the sting and smell of his first time with a woman in Boston. There is a bellow, as if from the belly of a beast, another, higher, strained, and finally a thin cry; the child has arrived.

◆

Twenty yards behind the dog sled, Buchan pauses to take a breath. Finished as a seaman, he's not even sure he'll even make it as a landlubber. He leans against a pine and pants in great clouds. Up ahead, the travois with its precious cargo slides to a halt. Ernst holds the dog by its neck, pushing his gloved fingers through its thick fur. Hannah, as Buchan calls her, unable to pronounce her native name, rearranges the blankets around their baby.

"Yer a mad bastard, Ernst," Buchan calls out. "God shits on us. He tips our boat into the sea, makes a limping fool of me, and tempts you to sin with this heathen. Why would you want to present your child to him?"

Ernst has heard all this before. "You didn't have to come. I would have sent a boat back for you in the spring."

"God damn you, Ernst. God take your child and damn you." Buchan yearns for a tot of rum, a baked potato, and the flesh of a red-headed Irish girl. Unlike Ernst, he could never touch one of those soulless animals.

◆

"You will respect my wishes," says my grandfather, "or you will have no part of my fortune."

I stare at the meat on my plate. "Surely, sir, there must be another way."

"There is but one other, the way I did it, and I should not wish that on any man. But there is no substitute for experience, and, until you have that experience, I do not consider you a fit man, Harvard degree or not, to take over from me when I pass to the next world," and then in a whisper, "whatever that might be." He pushes himself back from the table and wheels himself round to where I sit. "Listen," he says, motioning with the stump of his leg, and once again tells me the tale of how the wolves attacked him and my grandfather in the snow, except this time he starts further back, and this time it is the truth.

♦

Away from the bloody site of the ambush, Buchan has found a cave. There are signs that a bear was here, piles of leaves and grass, the bones of small animals and above all the raw smell of a thousand wet dogs. He cradles the small boy in his arms and sings softly to him of the sea. It is still day and there is a soft reflected glow from the snow in the narrow mouth of the shelter. Outside, some way off, wolves spit and growl over the body of Ernst and nose through the remains of the sled. One of them pisses on the carcass of the dog whilst others sit at the base of a tree, occasionally standing on their hind legs and stretching up the trunk towards where Hannah clings on and weeps. When the night comes she will freeze to death. Eventually the wolves leave in search of other prey.

♦

The sun has only just risen, but Buchan is already outside, the small Ernest strapped to his back, pacified with a strip of dried meat. Gingerly he steps out across the snow; he has been practising for some days now, but a mistake could be fatal. Especially if the wolves return. Each stride is more deliberate, and the work is tiring, lifting the snowshoe higher, tilting back on the descents, kicking into the snow on the climbs. He leans on the pole he fashioned from the broken sled. The axe is looped into his belt, its blade tarnished, and its haft splashed with dark stains. He breathes in through the mouth and out through the nose, to avoid the drips, but still his beard freezes up. With each step he feels a grinding in his bad leg; he sings, the pain his beat:

> When Buchan's ashore he beats his way
> Towards some boarding-house:
> He's welcome in with his rum and gin,
> And he's fed with pork and scouse:

The low sun is his guide, and at night he digs a hole with a scoop, into which he and Ernest snuggle. He is father and mother to the boy. He chews jerky, moistened with melt water, into a slimy pulp which the boy sucks up enthusiastically.

♦

One week out, and the last of the old jerky is gone. In the snow hole, clutched against Buchan's chest, the child is crying. Water drips down the slick walls and slides down the run-off, which Buchan has learned to fashion after waking the first morning in a puddle. The new jerky is paler and unseasoned, dried by hanging overnight in the freezing air, something the darkies did. The strips are uneven; some thicker than others, some paler. Still Buchan hesitates, and still the child cries. Holding the strip at the very end he puts it near the child's face. A small warm hand comes up in the darkness and pulls the food closer. The crying stops, and a contented sucking starts. Buchan gropes for another strip and starts to chew.

♦

"Why me?" I ask.

"You are all that I have." He scowls. "God damn your father."

"Is this why he left?"

"It is not as if he hadn't…"

"He refused your terms?"

"He refused to understand the truth. The truth on which my fortune was built." He slams his hand on the table. The servant looks up from the back of the room but knows not to interfere. "When I got back to Boston, I started a new company. I would employ anyone, man or woman, white, darkie, yellow even. You know, my first paymaster was a Chinee, a woman? Clever lass, died only last year," he shakes his head. "Had a house up on the Heights. It's what they do that matters, not the fashion of the trappings. It was out there in the snow, with your father on my back, that I learned the lesson. The lesson that he and his parents taught me." He picks up the fork and hands it to me. "All people are equal. They all taste the same."

Reading the Signs

Ramsey Campbell

When Vernon came to a roundabout with no diversion sign, he saw he'd gone wrong. He lowered his window in the hope of hearing where the motorway was, but the night was as silent as the February sky that looked close to sagging onto the roofs of all five streets. He drove back to the last sign, which stood on another roundabout, and then he noticed what he'd previously overlooked. The four metal legs supporting the sign had gouged erratic tracks through the dewy grass. Plainly someone had thought it would be fun to move the sign.

Five roads met at this intersection too. Vernon had been driving for at least ten minutes through the moorland town, and surely he ought to be close to the route back to the motorway. He might have phoned Emma to say he was delayed, except that she was generally asleep by midnight; he hoped she was now. Instead he turned along the road between the pair he'd already followed. If it didn't bring him to a sign, he would come back.

The terraced streets were deserted. The low sky appeared to have squashed every colour besides grey out of the ranks of narrow houses. The wan glare of the streetlamps blackened the window frames and the curtains that blinded the panes, the front doors that opened onto the street. He glimpsed movement among the vehicles parked half on the pavement, but it was only a cloud of fumes seeping from under the hood of a car. Beyond the car the road bent sharply, and when it straightened, he saw somebody trudging ahead.

Even from several hundred yards away, Vernon saw the walker was unusually tall. As he put on speed for fear that the man might turn aside before Vernon could ask for directions, he became aware that the fellow's head was disconcertingly small. It turned to peer towards the car, and the upper portion of the body slipped askew. The light of the next streetlamp found it as it righted itself, and Vernon realised that a child was perched on the man's shoulders. He was relieved to see it but unnerved by having imagined anything else. He could only hope that he was safe to drive — that he wasn't too much in need of sleep.

The boy had regained his hold on the man's shoulders by the time Vernon drew alongside. The small face looked scrubbed shiny, gleaming under the streetlamp, and the wide eyes were alert despite the hour. His long nose twitched, perhaps with nerves, as his lips pinched inwards. The father's long face had been dragged thinner by the weight of his jowls, and his dull tired eyes were underscored by skin that looked bruised, while his loose lips drooped under a bulbous nose. In his indeterminately coloured suit and with his shirt collar open, he scarcely seemed dressed for the night, and the boy's outfit wasn't much more suitable — a waspishly striped jumper inside a dark overall, both of them a size too large. Vernon lowered the passenger window and shivered at the chill that met him. "Will this bring me back to the motorway?" he called.

The man sidled between two parked cars and stooped to the window, but didn't speak until he'd lowered himself almost to his knees as if his burden had brought him to them. Vernon heard the boy's hands thump the roof, presumably for support. The man's breath glimmered in the wintry air as he said "What are you asking for?"

"I'm looking for the motorway. I was wondering if I've gone wrong."

If the man seemed unhappy with this, perhaps that was his

habitual condition — the flatness of his voice would be a local trait. As the boy's hands clutched at his shoulders, he gave the road ahead a dull glance. "You're no more wrong than me."

"We were going that way, weren't we?" The boy's voice was shrill and rendered tinny by the roof. "You have to say," he said.

The skin beneath the man's eyes twitched while his lips chafed each other. No doubt he was embarrassed to be prompted to hitch. "Look for a lift by all means," Vernon said, and when the fellow's face grew blanker still "I mean with me."

The boy kicked up his legs, displaying trainers that reminded Vernon how much Tom's used to cost, and as the cuffs of the overalls flapped they revealed the boy wasn't wearing socks. "I'll give you a ride, son," Vernon called and told the man "You don't want him out like that at this time of night in this weather."

Even if this was presumptuous, he thought it needed to be said. The man's face stayed expressionless as the boy leapt down from his shoulders like an acrobat. The trainers struck the pavement with a plump thud that set a dog barking in a house, and the boy released one of the man's hands. "Where you going?" the man said.

Did he think the boy was about to run off? The man had straightened up, and Vernon couldn't see his face. Perhaps Vernon had misunderstood the question, since the man added "You can't stay sat on me."

The boy's thin lips sucked inwards, losing any colour, as if his teeth or something else had pained him. "Would you like to sit in front?" Vernon said.

The man ducked to stare at Vernon. "Who'll be telling you the way?"

"I expect you should." Vernon leaned over to tip the passenger seat forward. "You do as your dad says," he said. "Better sit in the back."

As the boy clambered in, he gave Vernon quite a look. Vernon remembered earning glares whenever he told Tom not to do something at that age. When he pushed the seat upright the boy made a face, though in the dimness Vernon couldn't see what kind. Once the man had slumped onto the seat and fumbled the safety belt into its socket, Vernon said "Straight on?"

"That's where."

The man seemed to resent having to say so. No doubt he was as weary as he looked. As he shut the window, Vernon sent the car forward. Talking ought to help him stay wakeful, and he said "What's kept you both out so late?"

The man's breath clouded the air as he muttered "Broke down."

"Was that your car I saw back there?"

"No idea what you've seen."

Perhaps the boy would be better company. As Vernon glanced at the small indistinct face, he saw the empty street fleeing backwards. "Have you been somewhere good?"

"Playing."

Vernon took that for an affirmative. He tried giving the man the kind of look adults shared on the subject of children, but the fellow was staring dully through the windscreen. It was hardly polite to seem amused by how the boy took after him, and Vernon stayed quiet until the street ended at a junction. "Left?" he suggested.

"That's us," the man just about said.

From previous journeys Vernon had a sense that the motorway curved in this direction several miles ahead. The road he turned along was wider than the one he left but no less deserted. Cars occupied the concrete drives of houses frozen by the frigid light. He saw the boy's eyes flickering from side to side as though to take everything in, which prompted him to say "I'll bet my son would have thought this was an adventure at your age."

A shadow fluttered over the boy's face as he peered out of the mirror. "How old's that?"

"You tell him."

Vernon thought the man was addressing the boy, then wondered if he was. "Eight?" Vernon said, which was apparently an insult, given how blank the small face grew. "His name's Tom," Vernon said in an attempt to placate him. "What's yours?"

"Tell the man your name, son."

"I'm me."

"I'm sure you are and nobody else." Vernon made another bid to share the adult viewpoint, but the man was keeping his thoughts to himself. "I'm Jack," Vernon said.

Neither of his passengers responded with a name, though the man uttered a breath that bloomed grey. Vernon thumbed the button on his side of the car to ensure the passenger window was shut and turned the heating up to full. The man's gaze had begun to dodge back and forth as though he was imitating his son, and his thick tongue poked his lips apart. "Time to play," he said.

The boy sat forward. "Try telling, pop," he said and grinned as if he was no less proud of his teeth than of the answer.

"Sit back, son," Vernon told him. "You need to put your belt on."

As the boy's face withdrew into the dimness, his grin was the first thing to vanish. "That's no fun."

"I can't drive unless everyone is strapped in. I don't want the police telling me I can't, do I?"

"You don't."

Perhaps the man's voice was so toneless because he didn't like to see his son rebuked, in which case he should have done the parental job, though Vernon felt guilty for neglecting to check the boy had used the belt. He braked and waited for the boy to yank it across himself in a mime of resentment. As the car regained speed he said "Time to play what?"

The man's eyes flickered, but not in his direction. "You'll see."

"If it's a secret, just say so."

"Don't be like that."

Could the fellow actually think Vernon was being unreasonable? Before Vernon could make his feelings even plainer, the man turned his head away from him. "See the signs," he mumbled.

Vernon saw the small head swing that way too. "So that's safe," the boy said.

In a moment Vernon thought he understood, but said only "Intelligent chap, isn't he?"

The man expelled another ashen breath. "Likes to think so."

Did he resent his own son's intellect? That might explain why the boy seemed somehow to be holding back, but Vernon wasn't about to be daunted from showing concern. "Are you cold there in the back?" he said. "I've a blanket in the boot if you'd like to wrap up."

"Last thing he wants," the man declared.

"It really won't be any trouble."

"You're right, it won't."

Vernon was ready to ignore if not to argue with the man until the boy spoke up, shriller than ever. "I'm how I like."

"If you say so," Vernon said but felt inadequate. "If there's anything else I can do for you, just let me know."

"No call for that." The man nodded at the windscreen as though to indicate he was leaving the subject behind. "I'm miserable tired," he said.

The boy was looking where the man had looked. "It's my turn."

"I believe I see what you're up to," Vernon said.

"Is that a fact."

It sounded like a question the man lacked the energy to raise. "Can anybody play?" Vernon said.

"Depends." Even less encouragingly the man added "Depends what you reckon the game is."

"I'll make tea." As the man gave him a look that might have been convicting him of feeblemindedness, Vernon found the next number plate ahead. "Owls own banks," he suggested.

"You're as clever as him." This didn't much resemble praise, but the man contributed "Our own business."

"Out of bounds," the boy said.

Vernon felt oddly relieved to have identified the game, as if he'd recovered some kind of control. "Do you play it whenever you're on the road?" he asked the man.

"Got to keep your brain going somehow."

"So you don't nod off at the wheel, you mean." When the fellow kept any response to himself, Vernon found inspiration on a number plate. "Weariness is fiendish."

The man thumped his forehead with the fingertips of one hand as though to enliven his mind. "What it's for."

The boy seemed to need no time to ponder. "What I found."

Was the man scowling at his quickness? Perhaps it was up to Vernon to carry on the game, and a registration number let him say "Gee up, Trigger."

The boy's giggle was even higher than his voice. His father glowered at it, unless he was making sure his turn came next. He looked away from the mirror before he said "Get us thinking."

"Gone up there," the boy said at once.

Vernon had the odd notion that the game had turned into a dialogue from which he was excluded. He was glad to see they'd reached the edge of town. The houses ended several hundred yards ahead, and beyond them the road stretched into empty darkness. "Where shall I drop you?" he said.

The man shook his head as if to rouse himself or to dislodge some unwelcome burden. "Not round here."

"I thought you said you were on my way."

"Never said different. Not yet, that's all."

Vernon almost laughed aloud at the man's brusqueness, since there seemed to be no other way to take it. "So long as you let me know when you're where you want to be," he said as the last of the light slipped from the boy's face in the mirror.

The streetlamps receded while the moor loomed around the car. The long low slopes were in no hurry to reveal themselves, and even once they gained some definition the ragged crests were scarcely distinguishable from the drooping sky. Although they hid the motorway, the strip of illuminated road that ran between the sprawling verges led in the direction where Vernon assumed it to be. Otherwise the headlamp beams only blurred the dark that hunched around and ahead of the specimen of road. He needed more than the monotonous sight to keep him vigilant, and he tried saying "So what do you do, Mr...."

"Mister is right." Just as dully the man added "You've seen."

"That's what we get for being fathers, isn't it?" When his bid for good humour fell short of the man, Vernon said "I was thinking of the other kind of job."

"After one of them, are you?"

Even by the man's standards the retort seemed unnecessarily harsh, and then Vernon wondered if he was unemployed. "Isn't there much work hereabouts?"

"Here?" The man waved a hand so sluggishly that it looked hampered by the darkness. "See if you can think."

Vernon might have countered that the man didn't seem especially capable of it. Instead he concentrated on the lit stretch of road as it veered from side to side. A protracted curve led so far out of the way he thought he should be taking that he let out a dimly luminous breath when another elongated bend corrected the deviation. All this made him say "Don't you mind leaving your car all that way back?"

"Doesn't matter what I mind."

"Couldn't you call someone?"

Presumably he didn't belong to a motoring organisation, and the local garages would have shut down hours ago. Vernon was aware of talking for the sake of it as he said "I wouldn't like to break down out here and not be able to get help."

"Better hadn't, then."

"No, I mean if I did I'd be able to call."

"Not here you'd not. Nothing gets out," the man said with morose triumph.

"I think my phone would. It's pretty well up to date, not like its owner."

Vernon slowed the car to a walking pace and found his mobile in the fat pocket of his padded coat. As he touched the illuminated screen he glimpsed the boy's face blanching in the mirror. "Expect you've never seen the like, son," the man muttered.

Vernon blinked at the phone and brought it closer to his face before pocketing it. "I'm afraid your dad was right. I can't pick anything up."

"Want to watch out what you're picking," the man said so indistinctly that he might almost have been talking in his sleep.

"He's right again, son," Vernon said, the only way he could make sense of the remark. "Be careful."

The boy lurched forward, not far enough for the dashboard lights to illuminate his face. "What about?"

"Who you get involved with," Vernon said and glanced at the man for agreement. When the fellow kept his gaze on the dark, Vernon added "What they're up to as well."

The boy fell back as if the belt had recaptured him. If his father had glanced at him in the mirror, the man's expression was too fleeting for Vernon to catch. As the car put on speed once more, the grass and weeds that framed the headlight beams twitched to greet them. The dim outlines of the slopes shifted as a wind rattled the passenger window, emphasising the chill. "Would you really have walked all the way up here?" Vernon said.

The man shrugged as if trying to work off the last traces of his burden. "No choice."

"Well, I think we always have those. It's up to us to decide what's best to do."

That was aimed at the boy, even if Vernon couldn't have explained precisely why — it was the kind of thing he still said to Tom — but the man mumbled "Try saying that round here."

Vernon might have pointed out that he just had. He assumed the man was referring to the kind of life he had to lead, the poverty he believed he'd made plain. He was relieved to see a pair of headlamp beams sprout above a slope against the sky ahead; at least the number plate would provide a distraction. The beams groped back and forth as if they were reaching vainly for the lightless clouds, and then they fell to the road as the car appeared around a bend. Vernon sensed his passengers readying themselves, but it seemed he was the first to read the plate. "Three nice eggs," he said.

He heard the man part his sticky lips, but the boy was faster. "That's not easy."

"There's no escape," the man said and stared at the mirror.

The other car sped past, and the boy's face went out like a dead bulb. It was dimly silhouetted by a pair of red lights that shrank to embers before the darkness doused them. Vernon was realising how devious a route the other vehicle had followed. "This can't be the only road, can it?" he said.

"It's that all right," the man said without looking away from the mirror. "You'll see."

In that case it must be the diversion, and Vernon had to admit he wouldn't be unhappy to leave his passengers along the way, together with the tension they'd brought with them. It and the chill were afflicting him with shivers, and he was tempted to offer the blanket again. Perhaps the boy was inured to the local weather, and as the headlights revealed yet another extended bend Vernon said "Are there still schools round here, then?"

"Still."

The man might have been aiming the word at the reflection in the mirror. "I was wondering where he goes to school," Vernon said.

"Try asking."

Though this sounded quite unlike an invitation, Vernon said "Where do you, son?"

As the boy inched forward, the man demanded "Who's saying he does?"

Improbable as it seemed, could the boy have been taught at home? At least that might explain the man's resentment. "I'm saying he seems educated," Vernon said. "Literate for his age."

"He's good at that. Good at a lot else as well."

This seemed more discontented than Vernon understood. How could anyone deplore their own child's intelligence? He was determined to involve the boy now, and as the road straightened out further than the headlamp beams could reach he said "What should I be looking for, son?"

"Don't know."

"What sign, I mean."

"Sign."

Was the boy imitating his father to placate him? "For your village, if that's what it is," Vernon said.

"There's none."

Vernon wished he could make out the boy's face. Might the child be afraid to display too much intelligence around his father? "Your house, then," Vernon said.

"Can't see."

Perhaps he was protesting about having to sit in the back, and yet Vernon wondered if he'd misunderstood. "Will I know it when I come to it?"

"You'll be put right," the man said.

He sounded weary of the conversation if not resolved to end it. Vernon wasn't going to be silenced, and not just because chatting would help him to stay awake. "I'm guessing you're a reader, son."

"Reader."

"Of books, yes. Is that where you've picked up some of your way with words?"

"Here's where."

If he was trying to sound like his father, it didn't quite come off, and the uninhabited night all around them didn't lend his answer much credibility. "I'm asking because I travel in books," Vernon said as much to the man as to the child.

"Thought you were travelling in a car."

Vernon couldn't judge from the boy's shrill tone whether this was a joke, and the man's dull face gave no assistance. "The publishers send me around to show the shops their books," Vernon said doggedly. "A few of us still do that even with all the modern developments."

The boy leaned forward far enough that Vernon saw his indistinct face was blank. Surely no child could be unaware of computers and the Internet and how they'd changed the world. Perhaps, having grown up with it, the boy simply took it all for granted. "I've some books in the boot you might like," Vernon said. "The kind my son used to."

"He'll want none of them," the man said so fiercely that his breath glimmered with each word. "Nobody's getting out."

"I didn't mean up here. Hardly the right place."

"Right for some things."

Vernon wasn't about to enquire which. For several reasons he welcomed the sight of headlamp beams ahead. They ranged about beneath the clouds until the night appeared to cut them down, and he felt as if more than the dark and the huge smudges of moorland had closed in. Only the moor had obscured the beams, and soon they were brandished above a lower slope. As the lorry swung into view around a bend he grew tense, surely just anticipating the game. The headlamp beams dropped to the tarmac as his did, and he squinted at the registration number. "Call general assembly," he said.

"Child goes a-roving."

Vernon was reflecting that the boy had proved his point about literacy when the man said "Can't get away."

The lorry roared past, and Vernon glanced at the mirror. Had just the headlamps turned the boy's face so white? As the rear lights shrank into the darkness, the boy sank back as though he wanted to emulate them. Vernon didn't like to think the child could be so afraid of his father — and then a worse notion came to him.

He could only drive while he struggled to think. His mind felt frozen by the chill and weighed down by the dark, as if he mightn't be able to use it until he left the desolate emptiness behind. A wind blundered against the car and set the passenger window jittering, and he found he didn't want to look towards the man beside him. The dim slopes of the moor were trembling, and he wondered if the boy was fighting to restrain a shiver, just as Vernon was. He did his best to peer into the mirror without betraying that he was, but the boy's face had retreated into indistinctness. He was trying to discern its expression when he glimpsed a light ahead, and then another and a third — an irregular series of them following a line beyond a gap between the slopes. He didn't dare hope too much until the car was nearly at the gap, through which he saw more lights speeding both ways on a straight road close to the uneven horizon. They were on the motorway, and the intervening land was almost flat. He took a breath and swallowed, and then he had to speak. "I don't think I'm seeing a house."

The man stared ahead. "Keep looking."

"What am I likely to see?"

The man seemed no more eager to respond than Vernon had been to ask. It was the boy who said "Nothing you'd call one."

What was he trying to convey? Even by narrowing his eyes, Vernon still couldn't see the boy's face. He might have thought the child was trying to stay out of reach of the man's gaze. Before Vernon could think of a comment to risk, the man muttered "You'll have us for a way yet."

Vernon saw the miles of deserted moorland he had yet to cross, and the lights shuttling along the motorway as if to remind him how distant they were, and then he saw another light, a dim but undeniable glow on the clouds beyond the spot where the motorway disappeared rightwards over the horizon. He was sure the glow denoted a service area, and it prompted him to say "I can take you to the services, and then you're on your own."

He sensed unease so palpable it sent a shiver through him. The man raised his sluggish head as if he was confronting the mirror. "Depends what happens on the way," he said.

Too late Vernon realised he shouldn't have spoken. His first mistake had been to bring his passengers up here, where nobody else could see them. Now he would have been taking them among other people, but what chance had he left himself? Why had he taken so long to grasp how little the man knew about the child he pretended was his son? Not his name or his age, not where he lived or went to school… No wonder he hadn't owned up to a name either, although perhaps that gave Vernon some faint hope, since it suggested that the man might leave him capable of talking. Then the hope went out as if the darkness had seized it, and the car seemed to grow cold as the depths of a cave. The man had withheld his name before Vernon's phone had turned out not to work.

He was overtaken by a shiver so convulsive that his foot slipped off the accelerator. The car lost speed at once, and the man's head swung towards him. "What are you trying to do?"

"I'm not trying anything," Vernon protested, and instantly knew what he should. Using just his toes while he dug his heel into the rubber mat on the floor of the car, he pressed the pedal down. He let the car surge forward and then lifted his foot from the accelerator. His ankle and his shin ached from the strain, but his leg hadn't moved, and surely the man couldn't see what Vernon was doing. The head at the edge of his vision loomed towards him once more, and he didn't dare meet the fellow's eyes. "What's happened now?" the man demanded.

"I don't know. I'm not sure." Vernon managed not to grit his teeth at the pain in his leg before he'd finished speaking. He waited for the speed to drop so far that the car began to judder, and then he went down a gear, and another. He inched his foot higher, slowing the car enough to turn it shaky again. Before he could speak, he had to swallow a cry at the dull agony in his leg. "Something's wrong with the engine. I don't know the first thing about them. Do you?"

He hadn't said half of that when he realised how useless his plan was. If the man was able to fix cars he would have fixed his own. The pain made his foot lurch off the accelerator, and the car wavered to a halt and stalled. The man was staring at him, but it took Vernon some seconds to turn his head. The man's eyes were so dull that his emotions were unreadable, even when he spoke. "I'll give it a look."

"I'll need to open the bonnet."

The man's sagging face came so close that his greyish breath settled on Vernon's skin. "How'll you do that?"

"I'm doing it now," Vernon said and leaned towards the floor in front of his seat. "It's done."

He was unable to breathe until the man had sprung the buckle of the belt out of its socket and scrabbled at the handle to open the door and sidled in a crouch onto the road. The fellow twisted around in that position and stared into the car. "Shut the door for heaven's sake," Vernon urged. "It's cold enough in here."

The man slammed the door hard enough to shake the car. Vernon had been afraid he would demur. As the man tramped into the headlight beams, Vernon said low but urgently "Is your dad —"

"He's not my dad."

That was all the confirmation Vernon needed, and he blurted "What can you tell me about him?"

The boy leaned forward as the man stooped to the bonnet, and Vernon saw that the child's face was pale as ice. "Never mind," Vernon murmured. "You're safe now. Where do you want me to take you?"

"Over there," the boy said and pointed beyond the man, who was attempting to lift the bonnet that Vernon hadn't actually released. "Past all the lights."

Vernon was distressed to think that the child might be almost too scared to breathe; certainly his breaths weren't visible. "The far side of the motorway, you mean."

"That's where he got me from."

The man thrust his head towards the windscreen and thumped on the bonnet. "Can't get in."

"Stand back a moment. Let me try the engine again," Vernon shouted before lowering his voice. "Sit back, son. Hold on tight."

As the man straightened up, the boy did the same. "Have you got your belt on?" Vernon was anxious to learn.

"Never took it off."

How had he managed to crane forward so far? Vernon hadn't time to think about it now. The glare of the headlights mounted the man's body as he retreated several steps, which left his face harder to read. "Stay there," Vernon shouted and twisted the key in the ignition.

The starter motor rasped, and the engine emitted a shrill stuttering cough, but that was all. He felt the key grow slippery with perspiration as his mouth grew dry as ash. He mustn't release the key yet; you could keep it turned for ten seconds before you had to leave the engine dead for thirty more — and then the engine sputtered into life. He seized the gear lever and struggled to manipulate it into reverse, but it only jerked into the slot for fourth gear. The man was growing restless, swaying forward in the headlights, and Vernon realised that he hadn't locked the passenger door in case the fellow heard. Even if he did, what could he do about it? Vernon thumbed the button, and the door locked with a loud click just as the lever found reverse gear. The car lurched backwards with a squeal of the tyres, and as Vernon threw it into first gear to swerve around the man, the headlights illuminated his entire figure. His hands were jerking towards his face, and Vernon thought he was miming dismay until the man cupped them around his mouth to yell a solitary word. "Moorchild."

For a confused moment Vernon thought the fellow was giving his name at last. The hands sank, and he saw the man's expression. If the long face had slumped even further, it was with relief; he looked as though he could scarcely believe his own good fortune. Perhaps that was what seized Vernon with an icy chill, unless it was the sight of his small passenger escaping the restraint of the safety belt with a sinuous reptilian motion, or even just the way the temperature dropped with the cavernous iciness the boy brought with him. His neck was owning up to its length as his head swayed towards the man, who had retreated to the verge of the road and was thrusting out his hands to fend off whatever he saw. "He's yours now," he yelled. "You chose him. You're welcome to him."

He sounded hysterical with delight, and perhaps this was too much for Vernon's passenger. Before Vernon could flinch the boy scrambled over the back of the empty seat and slithered head down to unlock the door. He darted out of the car on all fours and leapt to his feet with a cry that sounded less like a child than a night bird. All the same, it was a word. "Carry," he was demanding.

Vernon had a last glimpse of his face, which was as white as the underside of a slug. The eyes dwindled as the lips gaped with a grin that reached around the sides of the head. The man had staggered backwards as the door swung wide, and now he whirled around to dash along the road. He hadn't reached the limits of the headlights when the pursuer caught him. Clothes flapping about its elongated limbs, it sprang onto his shoulders and dug its fingers into the top of his head.

Vernon didn't know if the shrill sound was a cry of triumph or the man's wail of despair or both. He saw the man flee out of the headlamp beams as if he could somehow outdistance the burden on his back. Then the man stumbled off the road and rushed into the night as the rider kicked his chest to spur him onwards. It was a game, Vernon thought wildly — a childish game if not a senile one. Quite some time after the figure pranced helplessly into the wilderness, Vernon managed to shut the passenger door and lock it, and eventually his shaking fingers let him control the car. He eased it forward and then drove as fast as he dared, because the lights on the motorway seemed as distant as stars. Until he reached them, if he ever did, he would be more aware of the darkness at his back.

The Boy by the Gate

Dmetri Kakmi

It was a rainy night, and the four of us — Ross Orr, Geoff Hitchens, Rebecca Nagy, and myself — had gathered round the fireplace at Rebecca's home to stay warm and keep each other company during the longest and coldest night of the year. As happens at this sort of gathering, what with one thing and another, people began to tell ghost stories. Real ghost stories. Things that happened to them or to a close friend.

As Ross related a particularly gruesome tale about a driver who encounters a grey woman on a lonely country road, Rebecca shuddered and, excusing herself, went to the kitchen to fetch more of her excellent chocolate cookies. As a tribute to her culinary skills, they were devoured in no time, and the plate had to be replenished, together with cups of hot Belgian cocoa.

Next in line was Geoff with an unsettling story from his childhood. Between the ages of ten and eleven, he awoke every night to find a blond boy standing at the foot of the bed. Nothing ever happened. The scene merely repeated itself, night after night, over many years, until Geoff was used to the visitant and did not bat an eyelid when the phantom made his nocturnal appearance. In adulthood Geoff

ıd of the same description died in that room
⸱s earlier.

ₑ-minded sort, I had nothing in the way of
.ions to offer, which meant I could pass the ball
ɩ hostess. Rebecca remained quiet for a minute or
aised her dark head and said,

ₗₓ   t happen to me. It happened to a friend long ago, when
she and I weɪe in our last year of high school. If I hesitate it's because
I'm not sure I have a right to tell the story to a group of strangers who
didn't know her and can't possibly appreciate the seriousness of what
happened to her at a young age..."

She trailed off, and her face clouded. Our murmured protests
and encouragements were met with an inflexible silence. Rebecca's
expression was eloquent. It said the story she was thinking of relating
to this comic gathering was no mere light entertainment. It had
obviously left a deep and lasting impression on her psyche.

"Come on, Rebecca, out with it," Ross, always the gregarious one,
said. "It'll do you good to get it off your chest."

She smiled sadly. "I doubt that."

The fire crackled in the grate, and rain lashed the windows as we
waited for her to reach a decision.

I studied Ross and Geoff as they sat in armchairs on the other
side of the coffee table and saw that the high spirits had left them.
Rebecca's disturbed mood pervaded the atmosphere and affected
the entire company. It was as though the spectre of a dreadful past
hovered over us like a stormy cloud. After some minutes, Rebecca
stood from her seat beside me, threw a log in the fire, and said,

"If I'm going to do this, I'll do it properly. You see, I found out
about it from a letter my friend Alice Kendall addressed to me before
she... before... well, before it all happened. I don't think I could
do the story justice if I told it in my own words. It's best if I read the
letter to you, if that's all right...? She was a talented writer; wanted to
become a novelist." She cast questioning eyes round the room, and
the three of us gratified her with a nod. "Excuse me a minute while
I get it."

She was gone for about ten minutes, during which time Ross,
Geoff, and I contemplated our own thoughts.

The wind howled outside. The jacaranda tree hissed as it thrashed and tossed against the windowpane, the bare branches flung about like the arms of a demented skeleton. A part of me wished to be safely in the guest room upstairs, instead of playing silly buggers with adults who ought to know better. As I said, I am a cynic and very skeptical about supernatural occurrences. It was all I could do to stop myself from laughing or sneering at the circle of glum faces.

I was about to announce that I was going to bed when Rebecca returned with an envelope.

"Sorry, I had trouble finding it," she said, reclaiming her seat beside me. She opened the envelope and removed several sheets of thin, crackling, and somewhat yellowed paper. These were carefully unfolded and placed in her lap.

"Before I read Alice Kendall's words," Rebecca said, "I should tell you that all this happened at Port Fairy in the winter of 1986. It's a pretty little town on the west coast of Victoria. Alice had gone there with her father, Barnaby Kendall. He was an academic, speaking at a literary conference. He had taken his only daughter along for a relaxing week at the seaside town. Alice's mother had passed away a year earlier." Rebecca raised her eyes and looked at each of us. Content with our undivided attention, she added: "And so to the letter. I'll leave out any parts that don't directly relate to the story."

She picked up the sheets and began to read in a voice that betrayed no emotion and yet provided the perfect accompaniment to the crackling of the logs in the fireplace and the shrieking of the wind outside. As she progressed with the tale, however, her voice gained a deeper, darker edge with rapid alterations in the registry of delivery. It mixed with the sound of rainwater gurgling in the drainpipes so that, by the time Rebecca finished reading, it seemed that we listened to a lament for the dead or a funeral rite. To this day, I shudder to think of it.

Dear Becky

On Friday night Dad was invited to dinner with people who are part of the literary festival. I had some stuff to do beforehand, so I promised to join him half an hour later. We are staying at a quaint place called the Merrijig Inn by the Moyne River. It's old and a bit run down but comfortable and it has heaps of atmosphere — you know the kind of place where crusty fishermen crashed for the night before going out to sea the next morning. Dad estimated that it'd take me about ten minutes to walk from the inn to the house where the dinner was on Regent Street, across the other side of town.

It was dark by the time I left. Port Fairy is a pretty town, with wide tree-lined streets and cute stone cottages tucked away in well-tended gardens. The thought of walking through the empty streets on my own didn't faze me at all. The guy at the reception desk asked if I'd be all right. I told him I was fine. The sky was clear, and a bitter wind prickled my skin. The air smelled of fresh brine and wood smoke, and there was a constant boom of surf coming from the back beach. It sounded like cannon fire. I stuck my hands in my pockets, hunkered down in my coat, and set off at a trot, virtually hopping from one distant streetlight to the next.

When I reached the centre of town, where all the shops are, I decided it would be quicker to cut through the churchyard at St. John's rather than walk the long way round to Regent Street. I know, famous last words. But it was so lovely and peaceful, and I felt so good and safe walking under the bright stars that I really didn't think anything of it.

I was standing on the nature strip, about to cross the narrow street and enter the churchyard, when I noticed something by the bluestone gate.

At first I thought it was a white balloon, hovering above the ground at about the height of a small child. Then I realised that what I took to be the light shining off white latex was, in fact, a face.

A boy's face.

I was startled at first and then intrigued.

He was incredibly pale and rigid as a statue. I was thinking a kid that young shouldn't be out on his own at this time of night, when I noticed his clothes. He wore an ill-fitting, old-fashioned jacket; heavy three-quarter length pants tucked in thick socks; and scuffed boots that were too big for him. His hair was dirty blond and messy.

Even as I stared at him, I could tell he was no ordinary boy. He was too still and vivid for that, as though he was some kind of high-fidelity projection put on freeze-frame. He even juddered a little at the edges, *as though someone had paused a video. I was about to say* Hello *to him when he turned and not so much as walked but glided very rapidly behind the gatepost into the churchyard.*

"Hey, don't go in there," I called. "It's dark." I ran after him, but he was nowhere in sight. He completely vanished. A quick search yielded nothing.

I didn't tell Dad. Next morning, straight after breakfast at eight thirty, I ran across town to the church, and there was the boy, waiting. In cold streaming sunlight that fell in dapples through the tree canopy, dressed in the same clothes, and standing at exactly the same spot, as if he'd been there all night.

The street was deserted; the houses closed up. I stood on the wet nature strip and studied his bloodless face. There was no indication that he saw me. The pale blue eyes seemed impossibly remote, as if he saw beyond this world into an altogether different plane. After a minute, in repetition of the previous night, he pivoted on the spot and disappeared behind the gatepost. Only this time, in daylight, I noticed something peculiar about the way he moved. It was as if he were a figure on a cuckoo clock, being shunted out on the axis of a mechanical arm and then whipped back again. It was alarming and frightening, too, because it robbed him of any humanity.

I searched the church grounds for a long time. There was nothing to find and, on the wide-open lawn, no place for him to hide. The church was locked so I couldn't make inquiries. A man stood smoking under a verandah across the street, but he didn't look like he'd welcome queries about peculiar children.

The important thing is, Becky, I wasn't afraid. Just puzzled. The poor thing looked so sad and lonely, and I wanted to help. I was convinced he was trapped on that spot for some reason, repeating the same action over and over again. For all eternity. Who knew how long he'd been there?

It was up to me to break the spell and free him.

At ten o' clock I went to a nearby bookshop and spoke to a woman with a black ponytail and beautiful silvery eyes. Her name was Jo. She was understandably perplexed by the story and said that, as far as she knew, no one had seen anything of that description in the churchyard. All the same, she picked a history of Port Fairy from a nearby bookshelf and leafed through it.

"Here," she said after consulting several dusty books, "listen to this…"

It turns out George O'Dowd, a fisherman, saw the boy by the gate in 1876. Marilyn McNally made the next sighting in 1916. The final recorded sighting was in 1946. The witness was Tony Wright, a war veteran who lived behind the church in Barclay Street. In all cases, Jo read from the book, the witnesses reported that the boy ducked into the churchyard and vanished.

I asked Jo if there were any theories about who the boy might be. She read from the book.

'Many believed the ghostly boy was Davey Adair, a nine-year-old orphan who did odd jobs around town in the early 1860s. It was a severe winter. One night the boy sought shelter inside St. John's church. A heartless caretaker turned him out. Next morning, Davey was found frozen solid beside the Barclay Street gate. In death he received what was denied him in life. His young body was buried in consecrated ground just inside the gate.'

"Here, look," Jo said and pointed at an ink drawing on one page.

At one stage the faithful were buried in St. John's churchyard. What is now a nice green lawn was once filled with tombstones, leaning every which way.

"What happened to the graves?" I asked Jo.

She shrugged. "The bodies were interred and moved to the Port Fairy Cemetery on the other side of the highway."

"Davey too?"

"Probably."

Despite the terrible story, I was thrilled to have found this much information about the boy. Now that I knew his name, I could help him.

"And I'm only the fourth person to see him," I said, trying not to sound too thrilled.

"I wouldn't jump to conclusions," Jo mumbled, her eyes still on the book. "They're only the sightings that were reported. There could be others that weren't."

Good point. "Well, thanks," I said, turning to leave.

"Not so fast," she said, grabbing my arm. "The book says that strange things happened to the people who saw the boy. I'd be careful if I were you."

"What strange things?"

She shrugged again. "Don't know. It just says, 'Strange and peculiar occurrences befell the unfortunates who witnessed the apparition.' Please be careful."

"You believe me, then?" I said to her with a smile.

"Don't see why you'd make up a story like this." She was a very practical woman, and I liked her a lot.

That evening Dad had to attend yet another one of those endless dinners people are obliged to go to when appearing at literary events. This one was at the pub on Sackville Street, round the corner from St. John's church.

It was a bleak night, with the promise of rain. Dad and I were about to step into the warmth of the pub when I said, "Dad, can you give me a minute? I want to check on something," and before he answered I ran the few metres to Barclay Street and up to the church gates.

Davey Adair was waiting for me in his usual spot, as unnervingly still as ever. In the wan electric light that filtered through the thick canopy of trees, he seemed to be made of crackling frost.

I kneeled on the grass and stretched out my hands.

"Davey Adair," I said in my best voice. "My name is Alice. I'm your friend. Please let me help you, if I can."

There was no response or even a flicker of awareness. Except that the juddering round his figure intensified. Then again he pivoted on the spot like a mechanical toy on a spring and merged with the greater darkness behind the gate.

Disappointed, I ran back to Dad. I was at the corner of Barclay Street when I stopped and, for some reason, looked back at the church. Davey Adair's shiny moon-like face poked out and studied me from behind the bluestone wall.

"Good," I thought. "I got through to you."

When I reached my ever-patient father at the pub door, Davey stood at the corner of Barclay and Bank Streets, staring at me. Even though I knew he didn't mean any harm, it was a bit unnerving. His pupils looked as if they'd been painted on his eyelids.

"Who's the boy?" Dad asked.

"Oh, no one," I said, pushing him inside.

He gave me a knowing look and left it at that.

That was four hours ago, dear Becky, my bestest friend in the world. I'm now in my room at the Merrijig Inn, writing this letter to you. Dad is asleep next door. The rain is pelting down, and the gale coming off the ocean is enough to put the wind up Captain Ahab.

Becky, something has been scratching at the window for a half hour.

I daren't look. The room is upstairs on the first floor. It can only be a branch from the big tree outside. Even so, I'm spooked.

Davey was on the street when Dad and I returned to the inn tonight. I caught sight of him as we came in the front door, and then I saw him again from my window. He stood under the streetlight on the opposite pavement, looking up at me. That little head tilted up. The pale throat exposed. The mouth moving as if forming words. But of course from this distance, I couldn't hear a thing. I must admit the idea that he followed me is freaking me out a bit. And then getting a glimpse of that mouth contorting in that awful way, as if he's forgotten how to perform perfectly normal bodily functions, gave me the serious heebie-jeebies.

I'm sitting at the small desk, wondering what I got myself into.

Becky, when the mouth opened, it was just a black hole that went all the way to the centre of his being. Poor thing. It started to rain, and the water fell into his open mouth as if it were a well or a bucket or something. He didn't seem to notice.

There's that horrible scritch-scratch of busy little hands at the window again.

Scritch-scratch; scritch-scratch.

It sounds like broken nails being dragged against glass. And it's driving me insane.

When I look up from the letter, I see over the well-made bed to the window with the pretty lace curtains gathered at the side. It's not a large room. It's quite small actually, built into the attic, with a dormer window, which is why I can clearly see Davey Adair floating, yes, floating one floor up, outside the rain-streaked glass. The hair is plastered to his forehead, and one hand reaches out to press the window. He reminds me of an abandoned puppy, begging to be let in.

All the same, it's a terrifying sight. And yet, for some reason, I feel so terribly sorry for him. My heart goes out to him. It almost breaks at the pitiful sight of him out there, alone and abandoned. He looks how I felt after Mum died. Shattered and lost and bewildered and in need of a friend.

Maybe that's what he wants, Becky. A friend.

If only his eyes weren't so lifeless. I'd fling open the window and say Come in, Davey, come in. I'll take care of you. You can stay with me forever.

His mouth moved again. I think he's trying to tell me something. If only it wasn't so black, like the coal chute at my grandmother's place.

All right. I've made up my mind. I've been sitting here for the longest time, trying to decide what to do. Now I know.

Hold on, Becky. I'm going to lay down the pen and open the window. I can't stand that scratching any more. And I must hear what he has to say. Hopefully he'll stop making that keening noise once he's out of the cold and in this warm, bright room.

I'm putting down the pen now, Becky. Wait for me, won't you? I'll be back in a tick…

Rebecca set the letter on the coffee table and looked up. There were tears in her eyes.

"She never came back," she said in a choked voice.

Ross leaned forward and said, "That's it?"

"Yes. She didn't finish the letter."

"But what happened to Alice?" Ross pursued.

Rebecca stared at the wall behind him and shrugged. "She disappeared. Hasn't been seen since. Next morning her father alerted the police. There was an investigation. Nothing was found, and, of course, everyone dismissed the letter as pure fantasy.

"The only sighting — if you can call it that — came late the next morning. A parishioner on the way to church found a pair of shoes embedded in the ground just inside St. John's gates. Turned out they belonged to Alice. Poor Barnaby Kendall returned to Melbourne with his daughter's suitcase and a pair of crushed, muddied shoes. He died of sorrow not long after, believing he'd taken his daughter to her death."

"What do you mean 'embedded'?" Ross asked. For a sensitive man, he could be callous at times.

Rebecca sipped her cocoa before answering. "Just that. The shoes were half buried in the soil, toes first, like someone was trying to bury them."

Ross whistled between his teeth and said, "Or like something dragged her under the ground, and the shoes came off with the force of the impact."

Rebecca grimaced. "Don't. That's too horrible."

"There was no evidence in her room at the inn?" Ross relentlessly pursued his line of inquiry.

Rebecca shook her head. "The window to Alice's room was open. The rain got in and made a mess of the place. This letter was almost soaked through. The police said she'd probably run away with the boy her father had seen, but I don't know… She wasn't the sort. Studied hard, got top grades in just about everything. You know the type."

"You don't seriously think a ghost called Davey Adair took her," I put in.

"Well, what do you think happened then?" Ross called out. His eyes lit up as if he was about to punch me for daring to challenge what everyone appeared to accept without question.

"I don't know what happened, Ross," I replied. "I just don't believe she's being held captive by a bugaboo. And now," I said, gathering my cup and saucer, "if you don't mind, I'm off to bed. It's late."

Geoff, who had been quiet since Rebecca finished reading the letter, looked up from contemplating the embers in the fireplace. "I reckon we should all go to Port Fairy and see if the ghost is still there," he said.

"Well, if you do," I put in, "you go without me."

"I always wanted to," Rebecca said in a distant voice. "I was just too scared to go on my own."

Geoff saw his chance and grabbed it. "What self-respecting goth would turn down the opportunity to see a ghost? Are we going or what, team?"

"Count me in," Ross said. "I'll drive us up there tomorrow. It'll take about three hours in this crap weather."

"You don't drive," Geoff reminded him.

"Oh, yeah," Ross said. "You can drive then."

"I don't have a car," Geoff added.

"I'll drive," Rebecca offered in a frustrated voice.

And because we are and have always been a band of four, I was compelled to say that I too would go with them to a distant seaside town whose wide avenues and well-preserved cottages have seen more of life's beauty and savagery than most places in Australia.

Maybe the boy by the gate claimed his last victim in Alice Kendall. Maybe he still waits.

"If nothing else," I said to Rebecca, "you might find out what happened to your friend."

At that moment the window casement flew open with a crash, and all the wild restlessness and ruin of the night rushed into the civilized room. A gust of wind picked up the letter on the coffee table and hurled it in the fireplace. Everyone leaped to their feet with cries of shock and surprise.

"No, no." Rebecca jumped at the fire to save her friend's memento.

It was useless. The letter was reduced to ash in a matter of seconds. Feathery blackened pieces of paper floated up the chimney and disappeared. Geoff put an arm round her shoulders and pulled her away from the gutting flames.

It fell to me to close the window and return order to the room. I fought past the crazily flapping curtains and extended both arms into the feral night to close the wooden shutters. As I did so, ice-cold fingers locked round my wrists like shackles and long nails scraped my skin. Startled, I let out a yelp and leaped back. In doing so, I caught a glimpse of the storm-tossed garden and the thing Rebecca's letter had summoned to this house.

"What is it?" Ross cried. He pushed me aside and quickly closed the window.

Calm returned to the room as though a switch had been thrown. The curtains settled in their usual place against the wall. Rain glistened on furniture. A palm frond trembled in a corner. Rebecca wept against Geoff's shoulder, and Ross stood over me, asking why I had screamed.

But I couldn't tell him. For the life of me I couldn't.

Nor could I stop hearing that awful scritch-scratching at the window.

Viola's Second Husband

Sean Logan

I never wanted to stay overnight at my maternal grandparents' house. Not ever. It was tolerable enough in the afternoon, when my mother and I would make that long drive out to the Lakeview house. The house itself was not equipped for a young person — it was all lacquered antiques, hard woods, marble hearth, grainy portraits in gilded frames, and, for the love of all that's holy, no television. But Grandpa was there, and he had enough warmth to make even that Victorian relic a reasonable place to be for a few short hours.

But I never wanted to stay overnight. If I did, I'd inevitably be expected to spend time with my grandmother. As it was on these afternoons, she and my mother would sit in the kitchen drinking coffee and speaking glumly about the sad state of cousins I'd never met, while Grandpa did his best to entertain me with stories and puzzles. Lord knew there were no toys in the house.

Despite all the hours they spent together, I never thought my mother liked her very much. She certainly never spoke badly of her in front of me, but they never looked happy to see each other. Even if it had been weeks since our last visit, when we finally arrived at the door it was a simple "hello" and maybe the faint whisper of a tight-lipped smile if someone was in especially good spirits that day. And my mother never called her "Mom" or "Mother" or any other variation of the word. She called her by her name, Viola.

I could hardly blame my mother for her formality; Viola was pulled so tight she'd make the queen feel like she was slouching. She rarely had much to say to me. She'd comment on my attire, but that was for my mother's benefit. "I see you're wearing your tennis shoes today. Don't dress up on our account."

I have no doubt my mother understood my apprehensions, which is why she never expected me to overnight there. Except the one weekend when I eleven. She said she had business out of town and said, apologetically, that she was not able to find another place for me to stay.

I suspect my mother had had a falling out with Viola. It had been months since we had visited, and when she pulled up to the front of the house that evening, she didn't take me to the door. "Sorry, dear. Have to run. See yourself in."

I hauled my satchel out of the backseat, feeling a bit sorry for myself, hoping she'd see my moping face and pouching lower lip and decide that this was more than any young man should have to endure, and she'd bring me along on her business trip, and I could stay in her hotel room with her, and we could order room service, and, when she went to work in the morning, I could go down to the hotel pool. Surely, when she saw my forlorn face, that is what she would decide to do.

But, no. The moment I swung the door closed, she raced away from the curb like she was glad to be rid of me. I watched her shrink into the distance for a moment, giving her one last chance to see my sad face in the rearview mirror and come back for me. But instead she turned the corner, leaving me alone on the curb. There was no place for me to go other than inside.

As I made my way to the front steps, I noted the foliage along the walkway. It all seemed more untamed than was usually the case. The beech hedgerow that lined the path was un-manicured, and there was ragweed intruding upon the gladiolas. Dandelion was peeking through the cracks in the cement, and the coral bark maple had dumped its leaves carelessly across all and sundry. The crepuscular light gave the scene a surreal lavender glow.

As I climbed the front steps, my feet clomping on the hollow boards, I noted the curling gray paint that crackled underfoot. I don't think any of these imperfections were well out of the ordinary, but my dour mood put me in a state to notice them.

When I stepped onto the porch, the wrought iron lamp atop the stairs switched on. Knowing I was seen, I stood at the door waiting for it to open. After a moment, when this did not occur, I rapped on the loose, rattling screen. Perhaps the light switched on because it was mostly dark now, coinciding with my arrival only by chance.

The door opened at last, Viola standing in the entryway, her frizzy gray and black hair pinned up here and there, her lips pulled into a small tight smile. If this smile was meant to make me feel more welcome, it was not achieving the desired effect. She was wearing a maroon shawl over her black dress, and, when I entered the house, I found that it was nearly as cold inside as it was out in the crisp evening air.

"Hello, Jonathan," she said. "It's very nice to have you with us this evening."

"Thank you for letting me stay over," I said at my mother's direction.

"It is our pleasure," she said as if it was nothing of the sort.

"Who's making all that racket? Who's barging into my house at this ungodly hour?" As my grandfather, dressed in his dark gray robe and slippers, shuffled down the hall, I noticed immediately how much thinner he had become since my previous visit. I felt a sad tugging at my chest. It was as if I missed him, though he was right there.

"Hi, Grandpa," I said and rushed over to him.

He hooked an arm around my neck and pulled me in. "Get over here, you maniac." He felt terribly frail. My grandmother, by contrast, looked positively robust. She was a very thin woman, but there was fullness to her cheeks and a general sense of fortitude.

"Have you eaten?" Grandpa said. "I made one heck of a roast for dinner."

"My mom gave me dinner before we left," I said, which was not entirely true. I made myself a peanut butter sandwich earlier, but I didn't have supper. I just didn't want roast.

"Very well," Viola said. "Let's get you upstairs to your room so you can get settled and ready for bed."

"Bed?" Grandpa said, incredulous. "It's only eight o' clock."

"If you would like to stay up and entertain our guest, you are more than welcome."

"I would, and I will!"

At the top of the stairs, I said goodnight to Viola, and she retired to her bedroom, where she slept separately from Grandpa. He had his own room downstairs. Years earlier I had asked my mother why they didn't sleep together like Ami and Papi, or like she had with my father. She said Viola made Grandpa turn the living room downstairs into a bedroom because he snored and it interfered with her sleep.

Grandpa brought me to the other upstairs bedroom across the hall, which used to be my mother's room when she was a girl. Any trace of her childhood was long gone. It was now a study filled with esoteric books on subjects I did not recognize and in which I would have no interest if I did. Her bed was the only piece of her that remained.

I got undressed and into that small, cold bed, even though, outside the bedroom window, I could still see the faintest coloring of the evening sun behind the hills along the horizon. Grandpa got into bed next to me on top of the covers and read from *The Lion, the Witch and the Wardrobe*.

"Have you read this one?" he asked.

"Yes, but I'd like to hear it again."

Even though it was more than an hour before my regular bedtime, I must have been tired, because I don't even remember making it to the end of the first chapter before sleep pulled me under.

The next afternoon, while Viola was locked away in her room, Grandpa and I strolled about their lush, overgrown garden. The old white Victorian and the thick clusters of birch trees that surrounded the yard kept the garden perpetually in shadow and gave me the sense of being in a tropical jungle. Grandpa identified the flowers for me, pointing out the oleander and calla lilies and hydrangeas — all names I already knew well. I often spent weekends at the botanical gardens in the park with my mother, and I had my own small garden at home, but I didn't want to tell this to Grandpa and spoil his fun.

He knelt next to a patch of creeping thyme and rubbed the herb between his thumb and forefinger. He held his fingers to his nose. I did the same and found it smelled a bit like my mother's spaghetti. I stood, but when Grandpa tried to raise himself from his crouched position, he groaned and reached out for me.

"Give us a hand, eh?"

I grabbed his long, bony hand and helped him straighten — or at least get as straight as he was going to get.

"Grandpa," I said, "how old are you?"

He laughed at the timing of my question. "Pretty old! Can't you tell?" He put an arm around my shoulder. I don't know if he was being affectionate or just trying to steady himself. "Actually, I'm not as old as I probably look. I'm seventy-two."

"Ami is seventy-two, I think."

"I believe she is. And I bet she looks a lot younger than me, doesn't she?"

"Why is that?" I said, though I should have known better. At my age, I didn't fully grasp the sensitivity some adults had to their age. Though, honestly, I don't think Grandpa would be counted among them.

"Well," he said, "I'm sure your ami takes good care of herself and eats all her vegetables. But aside from that, I guess some people just age faster than others."

"How long do people live?" If my handling of the subject of age was a bit indelicate, my bluntness around the subject of death of was positively graceless. But Grandpa took it in stride.

"Do you mean, how long will *I* live?" he said with a smile. "I don't know, but I'll be honest with you, because I think you're old enough and strong enough that I can tell you things honestly: I wouldn't expect it to be very many years more."

"Really?" I said. I felt a deep sadness at this, but even more I felt bewildered by the whole idea of life and death at that moment. "And what happens when you die?"

Grandpa laughed. "Boy, you don't shy away from the big

subjects, do you? That's a conversation you should have with your mother. People believe all sorts of things. Many believe you go to heaven. Your grandmother believes we can come back."

"Reincarnation, right?" I said, proud that I remembered the word.

"Well, yes, I mean, many people believe in reincarnation." He seemed somewhat flustered and ready to move on to lighter subjects. "Like I said, you should be taking this up with your mother. I think I'm ready for a nap. One of the great things about being O L D, a little walk around the yard is enough to make you tired."

I walked Grandpa up the back steps, then trotted back down to continue my tour of the garden, looking past the foliage to the soil beneath, hoping to uncover earthworms or banana slugs. I stuck my fingers into the cool black earth beneath the lilies. I didn't turn out any worms, but I did spy a potato bug. I followed it through the pink Gerber daisies and lost it behind a rose bush on the northern edge of the garden, near the storage shed. As I looked for the insect, I noticed that in the space between the old wooden shed and the yard's outer fence, there was freshly turned soil. This was outside the garden proper, so it caught my attention, and I thought this might be a good place to search for bugs.

I stuck my hands into the earth, and, when I turned it over, I was startled to see small white bones emerge from the soil, along with ash and dried leaves. This caught me off guard, but it only took me a moment to decide they must have been there to fertilize the soil. They were small, thin, and charred, like the bones of a cooked chicken. It must have been leftovers from supper that had been buried here for composting.

It all made perfect sense, but suddenly I felt very uncomfortable. I had the urge to turn around and look behind me, and, when I did, I saw Viola looking down on me from the upstairs window to her room. She turned away. Not quickly; she certainly would not have been embarrassed about watching me. She merely seemed to be through with me as the subject of her attention.

I continued to explore the garden, but I was continually mindful of Viola's presence. Each time I glanced up at the window to her room, I only saw her in profile, probably reading one of her odd books. But still, for the duration of my time in the yard, I felt the faint heat of her eyes upon me.

◆

My hopes for supper were not high. Somehow I doubted Viola would have pizza and sodas delivered. Nor did I expect her to produce a barbecue to grill us all some cheeseburgers. Despite the lowered expectations, I still managed to be disappointed. Last night they had nearly my least favorite meal — roast beef. Tonight they had the only thing worse — leftover roast beef.

Viola was down from her room for the first time that day, though she was still reading, sitting at the head of the dining room table, waiting to be served. She was wearing a long black dress, similar to the one she wore yesterday, only this time the shawl was a dark violet. Grandpa shuffled into the kitchen, bundled up like he was about to leave for the Iditarod, wearing a knit cap, a scarf coiled around his neck, and his robe over his sweat suit. I didn't understand why they didn't keep it warmer in there. This couldn't possibly be good for Grandpa, and, even though Viola didn't seem bothered by the temperature, she did have that shawl draped around her neck and shoulders.

Grandpa's nap did not seem to have done him much good. He was puffy-eyed and hunched over as he walked. He really did look much older than his seventy-two years. I did not remember my father's grandfather well, though I did remember him looking similarly aged. But he was an octogenarian at the time.

"So, how you doing, kiddo?" Grandpa said, trying to bring some energy to his tired voice. "You able to keep yourself entertained this afternoon?"

"Sure," I said. "I saw a potato bug and a squirrel and a whole bunch of birds, but I don't know what kind of birds they were."

"Well, good for you. I know it's not exactly Disneyland back there. Maybe one of these days I can set up a basketball hoop out front for the next time you come over."

"You will do no such thing," Viola said from behind her book. "The boy found a number of things in the yard to interest him." She glanced over the top of her book at me. I squirmed slightly in my seat. I wasn't sure if she was mad at me. She always seemed at least a bit disapproving.

"We'll see," Grandpa said. He coughed a wet, gurgling cough into his fist. He started to pick up the fork and carving knife.

"You *are* going to wash your hands, are you not?" Viola said.

"Of course I'm going to wash my hands," he said with mock irritation, "do you think I'm an animal?" He winked at me, gave his hands a perfunctory rinse under the faucet and returned to carving. He brought first me, and then Viola, a plate of gray-brown meat, small wrinkled potatoes, and a cup of tomato soup. When Viola received her plate, she closed her book and carefully set it on the footstool beside her.

As with the rest of the house, the details of the dinner table were uncomfortably askew with my usual experience. The heavy antique chairs on which we sat were too large, and the carved wood of the arms made it uncomfortable to rest my elbows. They were also too tall for me to scoot the chair into the table, so I had to sit at a bit of a distance. The table was set with a precision and formality that I found off-putting. Grandpa and Viola sat at opposite ends of the table, and I was placed equidistant between them. Grandpa had set my plate on top of a larger plate, which in turn sat upon three levels of scratchy placemats that did not seem appropriate for catching spilled food. The silverware was also too large and heavy. The fork and spoon seemed as if they should be used for tossing a salad. I could not imagine how I was going to get that spoon in my mouth to eat my soup. I soon realized I should not have been considering this to begin with.

"That is not how you eat soup," Viola scolded. "You do not shove the spoon into your mouth like you're sucking on a lollipop. You sip from the side of your spoon." She demonstrated, lifting the side of the spoon to her lips and pouring the contents into her mouth. It was a very small and delicate gesture. I followed her example successfully, but I found it to be an intolerably slow and unsatisfying way to eat.

We ate without talking for a time. I was very aware of the sound of my knife and fork clicking against the plate. I tried to do this carefully, because Viola managed to cut her meat in nearly complete silence, and I assumed too loud a clack against the plate would get me another lesson in etiquette.

As we were nearing the end of our meal, Viola broke the silence. "So, has your mother started dating again?" she said, without looking up from her precise carving.

"No," I said, horrified by the notion.

"She will, you know. She will get on with her life. It is perfectly natural that she will. I was married once before I met your grandfather. Did you know that?"

"You were married before Grandpa?" This was shocking news to me. How had my mother never told me?

"Yes, very briefly," she said, looking up from her plate, but not at me. "He was my college sweetheart. He was studying law, and he came from a very wealthy family that owned a law practice. He was going to be very wealthy himself in the near future, which meant that I was meant to be wealthy as well. But it was certainly not the prospect of his future earnings that attracted me to him. In truth, of all things, it was his hair at first. He had the loveliest long hair. It was wavy and blond and it went past his shoulders, which was quite uncommon in those days. I think he got away with it because he was English and being a foreigner granted him a certain indulgence for his eccentricities. For me, those unique qualities were absolutely irresistible. And, you may be surprised to know, I was considered a great beauty at the time. Together, we were the envy of everyone on campus. And shortly after graduation, we were wed. It was quite magical, really. But it didn't last. He drove his MG headlong into a rather large truck, and, just like that, I was a widow." Viola seemed to snap out of a reverie and finally turned to look at me. "But all of this is just to say that your mother will begin dating again one day and start the next phase of her life. I hope you'll be supportive."

I was surprised, and just a bit disturbed, by her story, and I wondered why she was telling it to me. She had not previously found it necessary to toss more than passing remark in my direction, but, here she was, spinning a heartfelt and very private tale. But then I realized, like many of the words she aimed at me, this story was not for my benefit.

I glanced over at my grandfather. His head was lowered, and he was concentrating on his plate, stabbing glumly at the meat. I wanted to say something, to him or to her, to come to his defense, admonish her for being so insensitive, maybe even make a joke that would make him laugh and shrug off all the weight that made his shoulders stoop. But I didn't. I didn't dare say anything. I finished my meal in silence and went upstairs to bed. Grandpa read me another chapter, and I pretended to sleep. I tried not to cry. I think I succeeded. He turned out the light when he left, and, eventually, I slept for real.

◆

Something pulled me out of my dreams. It was dark, and I was overwhelmingly and unreasonably afraid. I listened carefully and looked around the shadowy room with dread. I felt a cold, feverish prickling on my skin and a queasiness in my bowels. I saw and heard nothing, and my heart began to slow, but something still felt out of sorts. I bolstered my courage and crawled out of bed. I hadn't brought slippers, and my feet were cold on the wooden floorboards. It had been chilly in the evening, and the temperature had dropped considerably since then. I could see the silvery wisps of my breath.

I crossed the room and opened the door to the hallway. The idea of seeking comfort from Viola was absurd, but her room was right there, and I was apprehensive about going downstairs. Her door was open. I stepped inside. It seemed brighter in there than it was in my room. Perhaps the moon was on her side of the sky. I saw at once that her bed was empty. I glanced around the room to make sure she was not crouched in a shadowed corner. It was the first time I had been in her room. There were shelves from floor to ceiling along two of the walls. They were filled with books and jars and small unfamiliar plants. I also noticed, up on the top shelf, a lidded ceramic jar, white with a blue floral pattern. It struck me as something that would contain someone's remains, though I don't know where I would have gotten that notion.

As I was about to leave the room, I noticed a strange energy. It was faint to be sure, but it seemed to charge the air like static electricity.

When I stood still, I fancied that it pulsed and swirled around me.

I fled the room and crept reluctantly down the steep, narrow staircase. Whatever had roused me from sleep was unclear. The lights were off, and there were no discernible noises other than the ticking of the grandfather clock in the living room.

At the bottom of the stairs, I turned down the hallway to the closed door to Grandpa's room. It was especially dark here, away from any windows, so even the moonlight could not get in. I turned the porcelain doorknob and opened the door. The scene before me made my heart freeze for a beat and my breath catch in my chest. It wasn't clear to me at first what I was seeing. My grandfather was lying naked on his back, his arm hanging half off the bed, hand limp at the wrist. His head was lulled to the side in the direction of the door, so that, when I opened it, he was staring directly at me. Viola was hunched over him, straddling his frail body fully clothed, still wearing her long black dress.

Without moving, without so much as blinking his heavy eyelids, he said to me feebly, "Go."

At the sound of his weak voice, Viola snapped her head in my direction, a savage look in her eyes.

I scurried back down the hall and up the stairs, back into my room and under the covers. I lay there, shivering, waiting for something terrible to happen. And I kept waiting. At some point, hours later, I heard Viola return to her room and quietly shut the door. I did not sleep. I lay under the blankets until the sun was up in the sky, and mother finally came and took me away from there. It was the last time I set foot in that house.

♦

Grandpa died six months later. My mother said it was "old age," which told me nothing. There was a service at a Unitarian church in Lakeview. I didn't know if he was a member of the church; the priest who spoke said many nice things about him, about his generous spirit, that he was a friend to everyone he met, but he did not seem to be speaking from his own experience.

Viola sat on the opposite side of the church from my mother and me. There was plenty of room for us to sit together; there were no more than a dozen people in attendance, a few old work colleagues and friends from the Navy.

Viola and my mother never looked at each other throughout the service. When it was over, Viola promptly stood and left without a word to anyone. While my mother stayed behind to talk to my grandfather's old friends, I followed Viola out to the parking lot. There was a man waiting by a long black car for her. He was wearing a suit and seemed to be dressed for the service, so I didn't know why he had not come in. He gave her a kiss on the cheek and opened the passenger side door for her.

I sat on the steps of the church and watched the man with the long wavy hair drive Viola away. It was the last time I ever saw her.

The Devil in a Hole

Mason Wild

Father Guigal says that when the world was made, the Devil drew a long-nailed finger across the landscape as if it were a whore's back, and carved out the Ardèche valley. The Devil cut deeply in places, and, there, the water cascades; in others, he marked out gentle, teasing curves, and the river meanders; and, where he drew straight lines, the current is slow with treacherous eddies. When we drink together in Martel's bar, and the priest is in his cups, he leans forward and speaks of the Devil with almost Protestant relish. If he were not a man of God I would be concerned for his soul. But the rich red wine of Orgnac-l'Aven is heady, and as the Father says to me when he is sober, "Yves Montrevel, avoid the wine! Lay it aside, my friend. Your eyes will see strange visions, and your heart utter perverse things." What else does he say? That the white rock of the valley is riddled with fathomless tunnels, that Hell draws close to the surface here, and that a man is just a slip and fall away from tumbling straight into the pit with no chance of redemption.

This talk of the Devil, and of the ground riddled with holes, brings me to my tale. My work is not noble, but it is necessary, for I am the cadaver man. Wherever there is livestock, there is pestilence, injury, and death: a swollen calf with its tongue protruding, a sheep savaged by a wolf, or a pig with murrain. A limping animal is of no use to anyone, and bloated corpses spread an evil miasma that afflicts other animals, so the farmers look to me to rid them of half-dead cattle and even the occasional aged, loyal hound. All they know is that I take them away, and, in return, they might give me small golden discs of soft goat's cheese, a bag of chestnut flour, or a cured ham.

The Douleur brothers, two thickset village boys, heft the corpses, along with any unfortunate creatures unable to walk onto my open-backed wooden cart. Those which are lame but can hobble I hitch to the back of the cart, and Henri the mule and I take them on their final journey. Plump flies settle on the corpses as I pass around the village, up the monk's path, and along a dry stone wall into the olive grove. The path then works its way to the gorge where the tumultuous river murmurs and rumbles, then winds down a hill, where I stop at the chestnut tree that hides the entrance to the ruins. I cannot imagine that anyone but a fool would follow me, but it is here I scour the hills and low bushes for those who might discover my secret. My trade is a lonely one, but, like the baker's yeast, the butcher's sombre knife work, and the tailor's hidden stitches, it has its secrets. There are government inspectors who take a keen interest in sickly animals, and it is important that such creatures are removed with discretion from the sight of all men.

And where there are secrets, there are those who would steal them. I once boxed the ears of the butcher's son and sent him home squealing. His father did not confront me, as villagers might have wondered at his son's interest in the contents of my cart. The Douleur brothers are more of a concern — they know the rest of my business well enough — and I have had to take a switch to them more than once to discourage their prying. If I only had a son to whom I could teach my trade, but the girls now are more fussy than in older times, and they turn their noses up at a cadaver man.

When I am sure all is clear at the chestnut tree, I lead Henri into the courtyard of the monastery Saint Jacques and the final fate of my unfortunate cargo.

♦

One day in mid autumn, when the air was laden with the fragrance of olives and mulberries, Henri and I passed under the chestnut tree and into the courtyard, a cloud of brown feathers drifting behind us from the cartload of half-dead chickens. Lying on the birds, tongue lolling, was a yellow cur. The dog was wrong in the head, vicious, but his owner, Farmer Azoras, could not bring himself to kill the animal, so he drugged him, and I added him to my load.

Mossy limestone slabs lined the courtyard of the monastery, and from its broken walls grew scarlet blossoms and rich green ivy. Jasmine bushes shrouded the centre of the yard, and it was there that I commanded the mule to halt. I swept the foliage aside with my walking stick, looking for snakes. Henri has a steady temperament, but once in this courtyard he was bitten by an adder, and so is easily startled. My routine search calmed him.

Henri shook his ears, as I unhitched him then drew the cart around so that its rear faced the bushes. I felt the familiar cool breath of air which wafted from the white-flowered shrubs, carrying their scent. I tipped the back of the cart up, and the chickens tumbled down into a hole concealed by the vegetation, most dead, some flapping and squawking to their doom. The yellow-furred mongrel was the last to fall. It was into that nameless sepulchre I committed the cadavers and invalid beasts of Orgnac-l'Aven.

I fed and watered Henri, then sat back in the shade against the cold stone of the enclosure. I opened a bottle of wine, one of a case Farmer Azoras offered me for my trouble and my silence. Father Guigal had given me a Bible, and urged me to read the story of Job, so I pulled it from my pocket, but the warmth of the alcohol spread from my belly to my arms to my fingers, and they turned of their own accord to the Song of Solomon. I imagined the young lovers with their unguents and perfumes, their dark skin and beautiful jewellery. Some kisses they must have been to be more delightful than wine! I named and numbered Solomon's harem, and, like sheep, they led me into a profound slumber.

A terrible echoing cry tore me awake. The full moon stared down at me, filling the sky like an ice-faced angel, and I sat bolt upright, scattering empty wine bottles. One rolled into bushes, there was a silence, a distant sound of a bottle breaking, and then another scream, angry this time, echoed up.

"Stop throwing things down here, whoever you are, that nearly brained me! What's this! Glass?" The voice was a fearsome baritone.

I crawled over and pushed through the shrubbery to the lip of the hole. Someone had discovered my secret, or else… well, who lives in the deep places amongst the corpses?

"I can only apologise," I said. "It was not my intention to inconvenience you, Devil though you may be."

"What are talking about? I am from Paris," said the voice.

That the Devil was Parisian came to me as no great surprise.

"Will you help me out?"

"I think that would be unwise," I said.

"Look, I was hiking, and I tumbled down this hole…"

Father Guigal's sermons came to mind.

"You have been cast down to the earth, you who once laid low the nations!"

"I hurt my leg in the fall, and I think I must have knocked my head — it hurts like the plague. Look, just lower a rope down and let me out, eh, there's a good fellow? I have money."

"He showed him all the kingdoms of the world and their splendour. All this I will give you," I said.

"Look, I'm not the Devil. Don't be such a superstitious ass!" he said.

"Well, you would say that. Is not the Devil the father of lies?" I said, imagining Father Guigal nodding with approval.

The voice swore terrible oaths at me, cursing me for a dunderhead — just the language you might expect. Eventually, he let out a sob.

I certainly considered the possibility that he was in fact a man who had stumbled onto my secret, but it is best to keep one's options open.

"What the hell is down here? It stinks. There are things crawling everywhere. It's dreadful. Look, I am getting out my torch. Look down, and you'll see I am just a man."

He screamed again, and then I heard a low bowel-curdling growl. I leant further over the edge and looked down for the first time into the depths of the cavern, deep, but by no means bottomless. Far below, a figure stood in a pool of light on a festering mound of bones and bodies, in the centre of a vast cavern which gleamed and glistened like the workshop of Antoine's confectionery shop. The flickering torch lit huge wet caramel columns, stalagmites like piles of rotting pancakes, and, against the wall, what looked like a sugary cathedral organ descending out of my sight. Then Farmer Azoras's yellow hound limped into the light, facing the figure, who was clad in a dark tailored suit. He reached down to pick something up, anything, to use as a weapon, and a hefty thigh bone found his grasp.

The hound edged towards the Devil, and then leapt snapping and snarling. From the pile of corpses rose a black, turbulent mist — countless flies, sluggish from cold, roused by the battle. The torch spun away, and, amid the terrific buzzing, I heard snarls, then a thump and a crack and all went dark. Finally, behind me Henri brayed as if he had heard the hounds of hell. Perhaps he had. I calmed my mule, a worthy and loyal creature of burden, and one who would never betray my secrets.

I looked at my hands — they were trembling. If I had not drunk so much, I imagine that I would have fled much earlier, but the wine distanced me from the terrors of that night, as if I was looking at the scene through rippling water. I harnessed Henri, and we left that place at quite a pace in the cold light of the moon.

In church the next day, I was troubled by visions of the dark man, the leaping yellow cur, and the swirling clouds of insects. My stomach churned in sympathy, and, unsure of my state of grace, I could not face the Communion, or the wine at least. I returned to my bed, trembling.

The next evening in Martel's bar, after we had discussed matters of trivia, I gestured Father Guigal over to a booth to speak of the matter of the Devil. I trust the priest as much as any man, but my oath of secrecy to my trade is so potent that I must be careful whomever I talk to. And for a priest, Guigal has an inquisitive disposition.

"Father, my friend Clever Jacques, he thinks he has seen the Devil."

As is the way of our village, I spoke of Clever Jacques rather of myself.

"What made Jacques think he was the Devil?" said the priest, tapping his glass.

I filled it.

"His location, the manner of his dress, the manner of his speech."

The priest narrowed his eyes, and his fat eyebrows met in the middle. He knocked back the wine.

"Where was he, what did he wear, and how did he speak?"

"The Devil was trapped in a hole in the ground, his foot lodged in a root."

This was not quite a lie.

"He wore a trim black suit, blasphemed, and grew angry when Jacques quoted scripture."

"And had Jacques been drinking when he saw this figure?" said Guigal.

"Jacques had taken a little wine for his stomach," I said, "but he feels more unwell than the wine would warrant.

"No doubt. Perhaps the state of Jacques's mind has affected the state of his stomach?" Guigal smiled.

Guigal was unusual amongst his kind in that he was a doctor of medicine as well as divinity.

"Is the man — the Devil — nearby?"

"Jacques would rather not say," I said.

"If it is a man," said the priest, "then he is in trouble. If he is the Devil, then you have come to the right person. Perhaps Jacques would consider leading me to the man?"

I thought of the man in the hole, and of my secret.

"Jacques would be willing to lead you, if you agree to be blindfolded."

"Certainly. He wishes to go now?"

I nodded.

I ordered more bread and wine from our host Martel, who had adopted an air of disinterested condescension to hide his obvious curiosity.

Henri the mule was tethered to a lamp post outside the bar, slurping up water from a bucket. I hefted Guigal into the back of the cart with an undignified thrust. I hitched Henri to the cart, and, when I has finished, I returned to the priest, who lay on his back, his face covered by his hat, snoring and insensible. I thrust my handkerchief back in my pocket. I did not wish to disturb him, at least until we grew closer to our destination.

I trusted the mule to lead us well, and he did, and though he might have puzzled as to why he might be carrying a priest in the dead of night, the angle of his ears showed that he was pleased that the burden was no more than that of a small bloated calf. I stopped at Farmer Azoras's cattle shed, and borrowed a kerosene lamp, a long coil of rope, and two shorter ones, which I piled next to the priest.

As we reached the monk's path, low clouds began to form over the moon, and, by the time we reached the gorge, two great forks of blue light announced the storm, followed by angry beads of water which exploded in the dry soil. I clicked Henri to a halt, and I threw the oiled cloth over the back of the cart and tied it to cover the unmoving priest and block his vision. Henri, wise beast that he is, knows that the violent storms rage over the Ardèche in the autumn. What he does not know is that it is the Devil's passions, his anger at his stony confinement, that inflate the heavy clouds and power the lightning. Perhaps my tumbling wine bottles and corpses gave him more reason to be angry today than usual.

The branches of the chestnut tree whipped in the wind, its leaves flattened against the downpour. We entered the courtyard of the monastery, where Henri and I huddled against the wall for meagre shelter. The storms here are fickle like the Devil and soon the storm abated. I brushed the worst of the water from Henri. Then something prompted my suspicion — the absence of noise from the cart — so I peeked in through a knothole, only to see Father Guigal's bloodshot blue eye facing mine.

"Father — you promised not to look!"

"I only assented to be blindfolded. You did not make me so."

"But you were asleep!"

"I was resting my eyes. Do not fear, I will tell no one."

My secret was known, and Guigal could not unlearn it. It was not a secret revealed in the confessional, either, so there was no sacrosanct duty upon him not to betray my trust. It seemed to me then that many of Guigal's questions in confessional were to satisfy his curiosity rather than in consideration of my moral well-being.

"To the matter of the Devil," he said.

I brushed the bushes to assuage Henri's fear of snakes, then unhitched him as he munched on the foliage, and took the rope from the back of the cart, looped one end of it through the lantern's handle, and tied it off.

Then I led the priest by his arm to the hole, and we leant over gingerly.

"Hello?" I cried.

"What?" a voice echoed from below. "At last you've returned! I am hurt."

Father Guigal jumped back from the edge.

"I have brought a priest with me, so we can determine your fate."

"Father, please help me!" said the voice.

"Now take a look," I whispered to the priest.

I lit the lamp and lowered it down into the hole, and it painted the wet grey-brown walls of the cavern with its flickering light. Out of the darkness emerged the figure of the dark man, his fine suit shredded, kneeling next to the body of the yellow-furred dog. Its head was twisted over its shoulder, and its skull was crushed. The man clutched his elbow, and the twitching fingers were dark with dried blood.

"Please, help me."

The priest turned to me. "This is a man, no Devil, Montrevel. We must help him."

"I cannot move. I might be dying," said the man.

"Father," I said, "you are right. We must. He is injured and may be in need of extreme unction."

"I heard that," said a petulant voice from below.

"Do not fear, I am also a doctor," said Guigal.

"He cannot move himself, and only you can minister to him. I will lower you down," I said.

The priest considered his options, and a stream of emotions crossed his face, as if he were reading the book of Job. But his countenance finally settled on duty, the duty of a priest and doctor to an injured man.

"I am coming down," said Guigal.

"Thank you. Thank you!" said the man.

I looped the rope through Henri's pulling collar and tied it firmly to an old mill stone embedded in the courtyard floor. The other end I wrapped around the priest, under his arms, and tied it behind him. I tugged on the knot, and the priest grunted.

"That is very tight, Yves. I am not sure I can do this."

I passed the priest the bread and wine, wrapped in its wax paper, attached the lantern to his belt, and led the mule away from the hole until the rope was at full stretch, bar a few feet of slack.

"Just turn around, close your eyes, and hold on to the edge. We will lower you."

Guigal tested the rope, and climbed carefully down, holding on by his fingers.

"Let go," I said.

"No, Yves, pull me back up," said the priest, his resolve melting.

I wrapped the slack of the rope around a boulder, walked over to Guigal, and put my heavy boot on his fingers. He screeched, raising and flapping his hand. The other fingers turned white with the pressure and slipped off, unable to bear his priestly weight.

"Yves Montrevel, what are you doing?" he cried.

"Lowering you down. Your dignity is at risk."

I led Henri backwards, slowly, towards the hole. The rope scraped on the edge of the cavern, but I'd put it in a smooth cut in the edge of the hole so that it wouldn't fray. Henri backed up to the edge of the cavern, and I untied the rope, leaving the mill stone to take the weight.

"What is going on, Montrevel?" said the priest, his voice echoing like a sermon.

"How far are you from the bottom?"

"Ten feet, maybe more. Bring me back up."

"I think not, Father. There is a man in need of your attention. Are there secrets of the Church you would take to the grave?"

"Well, yes, but can we have this conversation at a more convenient moment?" said the priest.

"We all have secrets, Father, and I entrusted you with mine."

The knot was too tight to undo, so I took out my pocket knife, unfolded it, and sawed at the rope near Henri's collar.

"One day, even you will go down that hole, my friend. We all go there eventually," I whispered to Henri.

"What are you doing? Get me up! We can get more rope…" said the priest.

"Devil, you'd best roll aside. There is a priest on the way."

Guigal grabbed the rope and tried to climb, but instead he swung across the cavern like an incense burner in a cathedral.

"Keep still, Guigal, or you will be hurt!"

I waited for him to settle. He had become a sobbing, swaying pendulum. He let out an inarticulate cry of rage.

The first stranded of rope frayed and separated.

"You unspeakable monster! I'll excommunicate you," said the priest. The Devil was silent.

Then the last strand of rope frayed, and the priest fell and landed with a wet thump. Then Henri saw the rope coiling down into the cave, and I thought of snakes. The mule brayed, and a back hoof shot out to strike my chest. I fell backwards, clipped the edge of the hole with the tips of my fingers, and hung on, but then I fell for a long time.

♦

I have awoken, and I can see light shining through the mossy edge of the hole above. My leg snapped when I landed, but I cannot feel it yet. The Devil lies wet, unmoving, and the priest pants with pain and looks at me with angry eyes. Later, above, I hear the voices of the Douleur boys and the familiar braying of Henri the mule. There was one other who knew the way, and he has led them here. Then the light of the hole is obscured, and the corpses tumble down onto us.

The Whipping Boy

Damien Kelly

There was no water in the outside toilet.

A brick cubicle on the far side of the yard, it held nothing more than a bucket with a seat, lined with old newspapers that you brought with you from the pile kept by the side of the kitchen range. That could stand a few visits, if all you needed was to piss. But if you shit in the bucket, you had to fold it up and carry it out to the gully to dump.

"Even in the night, Pius. Yours are so goddamned dirty. You leave a stink in there, and I find it? I will batter you."

I knew he'd be on me later, kneading his fists in my guts, hoping to turn my bowels to soup and force me out to the bucket in the dark.

There was no water in the house. The chief reason for sending us to stay with our grandmother at Three Trees was so that we could do the walk up to the tap outside Swanton's back door instead of her. It was what allowed her those three or four weeks residence in the summer, so she could still legitimately call it home. Two buckets of water, twice a day; one to drink from and one for the dishes in the sink.

Potatoes we could wash in the rain barrel, and did every day.

Why were the Irish still in thrall to the potato? Even I, at ten years old, knew how the famine had happened. If it rained, you'd bring a basinful from the barrel into the long shed and wash the potatoes there. Crouching in the dust of decades-old turf, looking up at the swallows' nests clinging to every corner, and listening to them squealing at you; stuttering chirrups, like machine-gun fire. It was the summers spent in Three Trees that taught me to think of birdsong as just so much startled screaming.

The long shed, the outside toilet, and the empty garage that my grandfather's Morris Minor once sat in. They ranged about the main house, its grey face a chipped mess of pebble-dash mixed with crushed seashells, and lent it an illusion of stature. The tiny upstairs windows in the gable ends might appear reduced by distance, but, when sat by in the mid-dark of a summer's night, they were revealed to be positively monastic, with all the attendant chill of a stone cell.

My grandmother cooked on a cast-iron range, turf burning, and that heated the kitchen, so we all stayed together in that one room, every evening. My mother had bought a television for the place; a brand new black and white portable, with push buttons for the stations instead of a dial. But the number of times we actually got reception on it I could have counted on the fingers of one hand. I think that, maybe more than anything, the boredom of those evenings was what made a monster of my cousin Shaun.

◆

"Have you nothing to read, boys? Nor a pack of cards?"

I had Subbuteo in my case. I even had a pack of cards. But there wasn't anyone to play with. My younger brother, Leo, was ever content under the settee with his Dinky cars and a handful of stones from the yard to set in their way. Shaun and I would huddle on opposite sides of the room, though, him on a chair by the kitchen table, me on the floor in the doorway to the scullery, each brooding on the paint bubbling off the walls, and what would transpire between us when we went to bed. My grandmother would stew tea and reread the yellow newspapers that lit the stove and lined the toilet, and never seem to recognise the atmosphere around her.

"When you're at the shop tomorrow, see if they sell packs of cards instead of comics. Them damn comics don't last five minutes. Or I could give you a couple of prayer books. For poor sinners."

We three shared the big room at the top of the house. The thinking was that our combined body heat would make it liveable at night. It had been the girls' room thirty years before; my mother and her two older sisters. The older girls had the big double bed, while my mother had a single cot in the eaves. Now Shaun and I were the elder pair, so we shared while Leo slept alone. Ironically, Leo would have loved to have swapped with me. He adored Shaun, trailed after him, desperate to show the big boy whatever smooth stone or black, scuttling thing he'd just lifted off the ground. Shaun was all patience with Leo, you see, knowing how it stung me. But in this one thing, Leo was firmly denied. Shaun needed his entertainment, and wouldn't let us switch beds.

"Hurts even if I just squeeze them, Pius. If I squeezed them hard, you could die."

There was another room across from ours that had been my grandparents', but my grandmother no longer used it. It stood above the sitting room and was warmed in the past by the fire that would have been lit there — but the sitting room door wasn't even opened in all the weeks we spent there, let alone a second fire lit. My grandmother slept in the downstairs room my uncles had occupied, next to the kitchen and only half as deathly cold as a result.

Sometimes, I could slip out when Shaun was asleep, into the damp, empty bedroom across the hall and away from tattered dolls with painted eyes, the smell of the piss pot under the bed, and Shaun's arms. Shaun's legs. His sharp, unwelcome fingers, blunt, unstoppable knuckles, and the unknown hour when he'd wake. Of course, I was made to pay for flying the coop.

♦

"What were you up the tree for anyway?"

"We were getting long sticks to make bows and arrows," Leo answered when I wouldn't.

"Suit you well enough to fall then. I'll have to get a bit of butter to lift them wee stones out of the cut."

"I didn't fall."

Of course I told. My parents and Shaun's parents both would visit at the weekends, and I related every moment of the week's torments with breathless urgency. But all Shaun had to do was tell the very same story to make none of it true. Leo would be standing there, emerging from behind Shaun's leg like his very shadow, and the image of the little sadist I was trying to paint couldn't have been more laughable. This was what childhood meant, I was told. This is what boyhood was. We were as bad as each other.

So I tried that.

♦

It wasn't hard to do. Shaun practically breathed malice and resentment; you couldn't fail to breathe it in yourself if you shared the same air in the way we did. I watched him one morning, on the road below Swanton's where it dipped into the gully it had been built across.

He was catching the hens he had chased down from their yard by the wings, and throwing them as high as he could. He was trying to get them over the high hedges of fuchsia and rhododendron, to dump them into the gully. Everyone used the gully as a rubbish tip; tossing over their bags of household refuse, or pushing their rusty bikes and broken furniture right through the hedge, to crash and buckle below. That was the bad end of the gully, but it wasn't very much of it, and, for most of its length, it was clean and green, and dotted all along with natural springs. My granny talked all the time about how little it would take to tap them for the water we needed in the house, but nothing ever came of it.

I watched him then, the exultation of pure violence, and I could absolutely relate to what he was doing. So I ran, to join in, and he didn't raise one word of objection.

The chickens were used to being handled and didn't even try to evade us. A wing in each hand, bend your knees and flip them upwards. We never really had a hope of getting them the height of the hedge, but I could feel in my hands that it wasn't about that. It was the feeling of separation in those stick-like bones, the click you could feel under your fingers as the wing was stretched beyond where it was meant to. Knowing for sure that you were hurting something that couldn't tell you so, that was the thrill of the thing. This was the sensation Shaun had learned to tap into, to keep him interested long after I thought I'd stopped giving him the satisfaction of hearing me cry.

And that should have said something to me, it should have made me empathise with the stupid fucking bird in my hand, but I was thinking — I was always thinking —

I'm playing with Shaun. Shaun's playing with me.

"What the hell are you at?"

Billy Swanton farmed the land next to my grandmother's now that his father was retired, though he no longer lived with his parents at the house. He came up from his own place in the village at the Point, going back and forth between the two over the course of the day. You could hear him coming in the old tractor, but his first and last trips were always in the car, a new Datsun Bluebird, which was harder to hear. He'd spotted us from far up the road.

The first thing he did when he got out of the car was to lift the two buckets from the side of the road and tip them out.

"Now, get you pair of bastards back up that road and tell my mother and father what you were doing, or you can go back to your granny's and tell her why there'll be no water today."

Shaun was blank faced and silent, but his fingers worked like he was tearing at some invisible cloth. He only shot me one glance on the way back up the lane, but it made clear that our moment of shared sensation had been an aberration. It was obviously my involvement which had gotten him caught.

I'll make you pay, Pius, that one glance told me. *Somehow. And soon.*

And then old Laurie Swanton handed him the means.

♦

The Swantons' home had started out looking like Three Trees, but it had been radically remodelled over the years; now it was a split-level affair that looked like a bungalow from the side facing the road, but had a sitting room and bedrooms below, where the fields to the front sloped down to a cliff's edge and the sea.

Billy's mother, Maggie, was in the kitchen when we walked in.

It was a bright room, quite unlike the kitchen we'd come from on the other side of the gully. Yellow Formica and yellow wallpaper, all reflected by the stainless steel draining board up onto Maggie's soft face, where she stood peeling potatoes. The kitchen window in front of her was wide and looked onto the road — she couldn't have failed to see Shaun taking the hens in the first place.

"Are you that bored?" she asked us, drily. "My God, you wouldn't be bored if your grandfather was still living. He'd have found plenty to keep you busy."

Maggie Swanton was a nice woman. In her late sixties, neat and brown skinned, she couldn't muster the volume or the edge to truly scold. But then, she wasn't the person we had to answer to. Old Laurie Swanton, Billy's father, was somewhere downstairs. We never saw him usually, nor heard his voice coming from the house in the way we'd hear Maggie or Billy when up filling the buckets. Until now, we'd only really known him by Billy's frequent warnings about the man.

"My father will flay you alive if he sees any of you in that front field."

"My father will take his whip to you, now, if that tap isn't shut off properly when you're done."

"Do you see all those whips in the cattle byre? Those are my father's; he makes them. See if any of you set one foot inside those doors, he'll show you what he makes them for."

True enough, the walls of Swanton's cowsheds were hung all about with Laurie's whips. I hated them. My father had taken me to the picture house a couple years previously to see Clint Eastwood in *High Plains Drifter*, and I was ever after haunted by the murder of the town marshal. You don't shoot an unarmed man, so he was whipped to death instead by gunslingers — Bridges and the Carlin Boys — while the townsfolk of Lago, all in shadow, looked on. Laurie Swanton's whips were not like the bullwhips in the westerns, though. The whips on the byre walls had long wooden handles, some three feet or even longer. The leather thongs had been knotted rather than woven, long and thin. They were more like the devices you'd see in the hands of Victorian coachmen, designed for reach and height. Somehow that only made them seem more frightening than the bullwhips that had done for the marshal.

He was making one when we descended to the sitting room. He made us sit together in one armchair while he sat across from us in his, perched on the cushion's edge, holding a long strap close to the fire and knotting it while it was supple. My heart was in my mouth. I'd often had six on each hand from the Christian Brothers at school, and my daddy cut a willow switch that hurt far worse than the bamboo cane, but the knotted whip looked like it could actually slice through skin.

"Yes, but *why* were you throwing them? What pleasure is there in that?"

We neither of us had an answer. Or we did, but none that we would admit to.

He just wanted to scare the hens. I just wanted to be his friend.
Or —
He gets his kicks causing pain, and I didn't want it to be to me.
Or —
He likes to hurt things. And I could like it too.

More than anything, though, I worried that if we didn't soon say something, Laurie Swanton was like to ring it out of us. Wrap that whip around our throats and —

"We… thought we could get them to fly. A bit."

Shaun took my meagre offering and was quick to embroider it.

"And we were seeing who was strong enough to get them really high, to make them fly for longer."

Old Laurie didn't look old. He was still lithe, and though his face was lined, it wasn't jowly. The muscles in his forearms swelled and stretched as he worked the leather, like thick mooring ropes, coiling and pulling taut against a rocking tide of movement. He had the firelight in his eyes, and it coloured his skin as the walls of the kitchen had coloured Maggie's; each painted by their natural habitat, like camouflage.

"That's no test of strength," Laurie said.

The last knot pulled tight, he wrapped the tail end of the leather strip over a razor and cut it away. Then he reached down to a glowing coal and — quickly, but not as quick as I thought he would — pressed the cut tip to it, scorching and sealing the frays.

Laurie lifted the handle and extended it to Shaun.

"That'll test your hands and arms both, if you can get it to crack."

"Is that for me? To keep?"

"Aye. You use the big long handle to tap the cattle and turn them, like a rider's crop, but then the whip will reach to the front of the animal if you're stuck behind it. Takes a whole lot more strength to crack that, than it does them ones the cowboys use, though."

Shaun raised and flicked his new toy; hesitantly, experimentally.

"Not in here, now. Go and ask Billy to show you how to crack it. Pius, you sit there a minute, and I'll get another one for you."

Laurie rose, and Shaun rose with him, jogging to the stairs with a —

"Thank you."

— that rang with the relief he no doubt felt at not being on the receiving end of his new whip. So buoyed, he almost forgot to look back. Then, halfway up, he glanced at me a second time.

Somehow and soon, Pius. I told you.

A shaft of wood tapped my knee and was laid across my lap. Shaun's whip hadn't seemed as big. If this one was — as it appeared to be — bigger than his, it'd only provoke him further.

And you don't shoot an unarmed man, the cowboys said.

"No, thank you."

Laurie came round to face me, and I held it up. He really wasn't very old.

"You're the whipping boy then, are you?"

"No — I don't want it."

"The whipping boy *gets* whipped, son; he doesn't dish it out."

He retook his seat, leaning to scoop another log onto the fire. It wasn't cold, inside or out. It wasn't too hot though, either.

"The whipping boy took the beating for someone else. His greaters, if not betters." He sank back into the chair and only then did the seeming of a great age wrap about him, in a way I'd not perceived when he was standing. "Is that what the other fella is to you?"

I set the whip back onto my knee. I had the sense that this was the opening to a conversation I'd been trying to have for weeks, but I had no idea how to have it with this stranger neighbour.

"No."

"He does wrong, you suffer the consequences. No?"

"Not — not from other people."

"Really? I hear you're as bad as each other."

For a second my fingers were moving, looking for that feeling of wing bones pulled beyond their limits. Instead they found the knobby surface of the whip's handle.

"That's oak, from some of them big trees your side of the gully. His is only birch, much lighter. His has more spring, but yours won't break. It'll take more strength to get a crack out of that, though, the weight of it. But I think you want to carry more weight. Still, if you can crack yours, you're stronger than him."

I gripped it properly then, and stood.

"Thank you."

"I know, Pius, how it feels to be tarred the villain by someone else's brush. The only way to escape it is to stop taking the whip, and start carrying it instead. Show him you're his equal, and that you're not interested in playing his games anymore."

Shaun was at the byre door when I got back outside, Billy handing him back the birch-handled whip. It swished with a fine whistle when Shaun flicked it out before him, and, though it didn't crack, the impression that it could slice through flesh had diminished none. He positively grinned at me as the tip touched ground and all the fine gravel spun away, in puffs of dust like gun smoke.

I could see the standoff to come, where my whip would only help to substantiate his version of events in the inevitable aftermath. I might be the one crying, but we would be as bad as each other.

But I knew he was *worse* —

Show him you're his equal.

— so I needed to do worse.

I crossed the yard to where he and Billy were standing. I couldn't make it crack any more than he could, but my whip weighed more than his, and I was stronger than him.

It was the wooden tip of the handle that ripped through his cheek, not the leather knots.

Shaun was screaming his teeth out, Billy roaring at me like a bull. Maggie came squealing up behind me from the house. The blood had been a flash going off — like a camera bulb — now just an after-image in my swimming vision.

I had nowhere to run. But I ran. And ended up back down the stairs in front of Laurie.

As I held the whip out, trying to give it back for a second time, we both saw how much blood was on it.

"I —"

He looked so confused. "No."

Whatever else he'd meant to say got lost in that moment. Instead he looked up, right at the ceiling, and his jaw worked like it was on the end of a broken spring. When he looked down, his ruddy face had turned ashen.

"Ah, Pius." He took the whip and wiped the end of the handle through his fist. It came away clean. "You weren't — *I* never meant you to go that far."

I howled in panic, and my legs bent of their own accord. He stooped to steady me, his rope-like arms anchoring my body.

"*What am I going to do?*"

"It's alright, I'll sort it. You run home. Tell your granny that Billy is bringing the water."

He ushered me to the stairs, and I staggered up to the kitchen door, my bladder threatening to empty with every step. I could see Billy standing over Shaun; my cousin had his back turned to me, so I couldn't see his ruined face. Billy spotted me standing there and frowned. I wondered where his mother had gone — was she already on her way to granny?

"You're in the bad books."

Her voice startled me. Maggie was standing to my left; in her kitchen, still peeling potatoes, her soft face yellow.

"You may go out and face the music."

"You could have had his eye out!" Billy snapped at me as I stepped outside.

Shaun turned round to look at me. His face was fine. There wasn't a mark on it, though the blank expression — truly blank, not just well composed — was new. Billy and Maggie might not seem to remember what had happened only minutes before, but it looked like Shaun did.

"Away home, you. Shaun and I can bring the water."

When they eventually reached Three Trees, Billy was carrying the oak-handled whip.

"My father said to give it back to you — but see that you have a bit more care with it."

Shaun stayed outside the rest of the evening, apart from ten minutes spent bolting his dinner at the table and avoiding my gaze. I stayed in, avoiding his.

I didn't try telling myself that I'd imagined it, that it was just a morbid daydream. I had no alternative explanations, though. By day's end I'd resolved to believe that God had somehow intervened; that — like Abraham — I was good, but had been on the cusp of doing something terrible. I had been given a second chance. I couldn't decide if Laurie Swanton was an angel or just the tool to hand that God had used to teach me this lesson. I just had to hope that this meant things were going to get better.

I still couldn't face Shaun, though.

That night, just as we were heading for the stairs, I complained of a belly cramp, grabbed a newspaper from the pile and took off for the toilet. I sat long enough that granny came looking for me, but I told her it was easing. Then I sat in the dark until the feeling had gone from my legs, such that they wouldn't hold me, and I crawled back to the house on my knees. I lay on the front step until the pins and needles had passed, and when I finally went inside, granny was in bed. I treaded carefully on the stairs, and stopped short of the big room, opened my grandparents' old room instead and headed to the damp bed there.

Shaun had been waiting behind the door. With his whip.

◆

"Can you not stay in until you've had some breakfast at least? And why do you have a scarf on you? Pius? *Pius!*"

I didn't take the road. I didn't want to risk running into Billy Swanton before I could get to his father. I ran past the toilet and pushed through the fence, into the long fields that ran down from the yard towards the cliffs and the bay below. My grandmother rented them out for grazing, and the cattle began to turn and follow me as I ran down the side of the field, thinking I was there to lead them. I left them behind me quickly, ducking into the treeline that bordered the gully and down into the dark.

It might have been a river once, the many springs that rose along its length seeded by ancient waters rushing to fall from the cliffs. But the road had cut its throat, and the long bed was dry now. I planned to cross into the Swantons' land and up to the sitting room window, hoping to spot Laurie in his seat by the fire. Failing that, see if I could find a way in other than the kitchen door, as I didn't have anything more to say to Maggie than I did to her son Billy. I needed Laurie. I had to believe that he was the angel I'd imagined him to be.

My guardian angel was waiting for me in the gully.

"What's that scarf covering?"

I pulled the scarf away. There was no sense in being evasive anymore.

Broken vessels marked the points where each knot had dug in; a necklace of bloody pearls.

"With the whip I gave him?"

"Can you take it away? Please?"

He drew breath for a long time. I thought he would say something enormous, something biblical; something that needed an amount of air commensurate to its enormity. He must have changed his mind, though, and the how of my request remained unspoken.

"Why?"

The spring waters pattered on the stones, a fluttering heartbeat that echoed down the channel.

"I don't want anyone to see."

Laurie came across the gully to put his fingers on my neck. His hands were ruined by days working outside and nights working leather by the fire. They brushed my skin like hide gone dry.

"Why not show everyone what he's done to you? Haven't you been trying to tell them over and over?"

"But this *was* my fault. Because of what I did to him yesterday, before you fixed it. I *am* as bad as him now."

"Is that what you believe?"

"Believe?"

I'd obviously been thinking about what I was supposed to have learned from Laurie's actions the day before. I'd worked out that some test of faith was bound to be part of what was happening.

"I believe in God, I swear. And... I believe that everyone deserves to be forgiven. I do."

Laurie hissed through his teeth.

"I don't know what else I'm meant to say, I'm sorry. You're my guardian angel, Mr. Swanton, and I believe in you."

He continued to trace his fingers over my skin as I spoke. It didn't feel like it was easing any.

I'd come to him, the moment I could. He'd been waiting — hell, he'd met me halfway. I had no idea what further part of the bargain I was failing to satisfy; all I could think about was the urgency of the situation.

"Please — if he tells on me, they'll find out about you too."

"That sounds like a threat, Pius."

"No! I just meant that we'd be helping each other."

His eyes were watery this close. Not tearful, but drowned; seeping on themselves like the rocks at our feet.

Laurie let go of my throat. It hadn't healed. He turned and began to climb the slope on his own side of the gully, reaching up to the low-hanging branches to give himself balance.

"*Please!*"

"I'm not your guardian angel, son."

"But — how did you know I was coming to look for you, then?"

"Because I'm the kind of angel that knows when somebody wants something, Pius, and what they're willing to give up to get it."

He gave me a look, all in shadow from the trees, and in my head I was suddenly back in the darkened picture house, watching Clint Eastwood play the Stranger from *High Plains Drifter*. Hand raised like Clint's, painting over the sign for Lago and writing Hell in its place.

"Are you —?"

"Tell your granny, Pius."

"Are you the Devil?"

Another enormous drink of air.

"I was."

Such quiet. The springs stopped bubbling around us, and the only patter was of blood in the small organ of my fear. Then suddenly, they burst with bullets of steam. I yelped like a pup.

"I suppose," said Laurie, "I still am."

I ran again, away from him this time, though he'd shown no signs of turning back. I didn't know whether to run for my granny and beg her for the prayer book, or to run straight to the village and try to find the priest.

As bad as Shaun? I was worse. I was going to Hell.

"*Pius!*"

I'd made it halfway back up the field, following the treeline of the gully, and Shaun was dropping down from the top of the gate that separated the yard from the fields.

"Shaun! Old Laurie Swanton is the Devil!"

"Did you tell?"

His question caught me short, and I stopped where I was. "What?"

"You're not wearing your scarf. Did you tell old Laurie on me?"

He pushed away from the gate, and his hand came forward. He had the birch whip in it. He'd obviously been waiting for me a while, as the cattle had come to the head of the field to him. He tapped them with the whip handle to part the herd as he came towards me.

"Laurie is the Devil, Shaun. It was him fixed your face and took away all the blood, and I wanted him to —"

"What are you talking about? Stop talking shit — what did you tell him about your neck?"

Laurie had fixed more than I'd thought. I'd assumed the look on Shaun's face the day before to be remembrance of the real course of events, but it seemed not. What had last night been about then?

"Shaun, I swear, Laurie Swanton *is* the Devil, and he gave us those whips to make us fight. He egged me on to cut your face —"

"I *knew* it. I knew that's what you were trying to do, not crack the whip at all."

For wanting to hurt him. Shaun had strangled me just for *wanting* to hurt him back.

And then he raised and snapped his own whip. It cracked like a gunshot, just as Billy must have showed him after I'd gone. A heifer to his right leapt in alarm, and the herd moved with her as she moved back out of his way.

"Did you tell on me, Pius?"

He'd been practising. He must have spent the whole evening outside doing nothing else. He passed the whip to his off hand and cracked on the other side. The cattle leapt in greater numbers. He was pushing them forward alongside him.

"He knew," I shouted. "He's the —"

Another crack, closely followed by one more to the far side, and the cattle were jogging now, moving ahead of him rather than just apace. Skittish, ready to run. At me.

"Not until you took your scarf off."

And then, just as I had thrashed him in the face with the oak handle, Shaun swung his birch rod backhand with all his might, cracking it into the back of the closest cow. I had the trees behind me, and he knew if I ran that would only draw them on faster. He meant for them to plough me into the earth, to toss me into the gully with the rest of the rubbish.

The cow dropped her head, planted her front hooves, pulled up the back ones, and kicked him. He only took the one hoof to the chest, but she smashed him like a china doll.

I stood and watched him, bubbling like a crimson spring. Then he burst, like a head of steam — a red spray thrown high, as his neck and chest went into spasm. Then he stopped.

I felt the oak handle slide into my hand and turned to see Laurie beside me.

"Do you want me to fix it?"

I willed myself to answer; willed my dry mouth to move and say *yes, change the world again. Bring Shaun back to life.*

"Should I change what's happened, Pius?"

But I couldn't speak. I didn't speak. The cattle had closed around me, and I raised the oak whip to urge them aside and send them down the field.

"Maybe just this, then," the Devil said.

And as the cattle moved away, I could see my granny standing at the gate to the field, from where she had apparently observed it all.

"She doesn't see me," Laurie told me. "You and I are done now, Pius."

138

"Am I going to Hell?"

"I don't know. I don't care. I never had anything to do with that. But you're definitely a great one for choosing to be the victim, so I'm sure you'll find a way down if that's what you want."

◆

We came back again the following summer. Granny, Leo, and I, and this time my parents stayed too. Old Laurie Swanton was dead, we heard. Maggie didn't seem too sad. She was a nice woman.

There was never any water in the house. Their gully springs ran dry the year Shaun died. It put pay to any plans of using them to bring water to the house, which in turn seemed to signal the end of granny going home to Three Trees. She took her first trip to Majorca with my uncle the following summer and died at Halloween.

But that final summer was glorious. They worked so hard to make different memories for me. My parents opened up the good sitting room and lit the fire there, which seemed to warm the whole upstairs and not just the smaller room where they slept. We played in the fields with our whips, and there was Subbuteo or a card school in the evenings, presuming there was no reception on the TV.

But at night I felt ashamed. The daylight joys were whips to scourge me in my dreams. Whips in Shaun's hands.

I shared the bed with Leo now, and I would watch him sleeping when I couldn't. Even the hiss of his breathing was like the whistle of a whip in the air, which only added to my frustration. In truth, it made me angry.

Sometimes, it made me so angry, I felt like cracking him.

The Vault of Artemas Smith

Phil Reeves

It was with apprehension that I unlocked the safe I found upon Mr. Artemas Smith's destroyed property. All I experienced after that decision to venture into those arcane halls has been judged by everyone as nothing short of impossible. The extensive search by the police, once I was in custody, did nothing to produce any physical evidence. So now I sit, locked within a prison cell for trespassing into a citizen's home, with the vain hope that my account will be read by others who should know the truth. I attest to my own sanity, though the authorities have robbed me of all other dignity. I hold the fact of accuracy as the one characteristic that will convince anyone that my actions beneath Mr. Smith's home were duly understandable.

From his biweekly correspondence, I could tell of Mr. Smith's pleasant nature, detecting no undertones of singular horror or perversion. We had communicated for months after my father had given me his address for a subject I have unfortunately forgotten. I was also given a heliotype portrait clipped from the pages of a forgotten journal. The most memorable feature of Mr. Smith was his distinctive expression, but I wish never to see that picture again, and, if my property had not been seized, I would burn it immediately.

It is also understandable that after the lack of communication for near four months, I went to investigate the absence of my friend's replies.

i.

I arrived a little after five p.m. on November 9th, outside what I had identified as the address of Mr. Smith's abode. The edifice was possibly one hundred years old, nothing past that. The build was that of a detached two storey home a little over a mile from the city centre, with three rooms on the top floor and four below. What confounded me was how little was left of the vacant building; I observed personal effects scattered and buried within the debris, all somewhat eroded by the elements. The houses in the lane were all abandoned and half demolished, with nature attempting to reclaim the dull piles of brick and steel. The evening did little to shift my prevailing feeling of isolation, and it was at this point I somehow convinced myself that Mr. Smith would have left some message as to his move from his destroyed home, or even that I somehow had the wrong street. The former, a belief that was subsequently vindicated, although the nature of the message was nothing I could have imagined at the time.

A brief search of the house turned up no indication of the whereabouts of Mr. Smith or how my letters ever got to him, even if they arrived there at all. What I did happen upon, though, was a flight of stone stairs around the back of the house that I had not noticed from the rubble-strewn road. I descended and found a cellar that was far more intact than the rest of the building. The low ceiling was unsettlingly damp and added to the curious feeling of absence that began to come over me. My torch took little time to find the only item that seemed to have been left in the cellar.

The safe.

The thing was organic in its design, with the air of great workmanship. The maker was perhaps enthused by some unconventional oceanic source; reflected in both the curling scrollwork that adorned the face and the skilfully tooled lever. Large though the safe was in its volume, once opened, it could in all probability only contain a single man if he were to squat inside. As I passed my light across its surface, I observed a sheen to the metal that was wholly unsavoury, as if the surface was damp with a queer vulcanized texture. When a direct light was not upon the metal, it lost its iridescence and assumed a pallid grey colour.

Upon inspection, I established that the safe was locked, with no key to be seen. It was clear that after my earlier futile search of the building, the safe must contain the only possible clue to Mr. Smith's location. I discovered the key to the safe on the remaining southwest cellar wall, upon a hook two feet from the floor. Inscribed upon the key was the hallmark of the safe makers; this matched the insignia upon the vault itself. I stress again that Mr. Smith had not sent me a key to this safe or expressed where it could be discovered within his property.

The interior of the safe was undisturbed; but to all impressions empty. There was a large space between the topmost shelf and one at waist height, under which two metal drawers were closed. I pulled upon the cold metal of the cash drawers' handles, but with too great a force. Their lack of contents caught me off guard, for I heaved them so hard, I pulled them clean from the safe, and they skidded onto the concrete floor. I was about to give up with the foolish venture after hurting myself with the action, but I noticed that inside one of the drawers was a neat stack of my letters, opened, and bundled together. Perhaps it was this discovery that somehow precipitated the events to follow, for at once I then noticed a pull-ring recessed into the baseplate of the safe. It was styled as the vault, with no hint of the hatch being added at a later date. With the evidence of the letters linking this safe to Mr. Smith, I took hold of the ring and drew it toward me in the hope of finding more information. With little effort the plate shifted, and it was easily pulled out and laid beside the drawers.

What arose from the compartment assaulted my nostrils to such a degree that I near succumbed; the air was awfully foetid, and it swept over me in waves as I tried not to gag. I was then aware of a tremendous rushing sound; air was passing from the cellar into the hidden section I had opened. It was only then I became enlightened; this was not a secret compartment at all, but a passage going much deeper through the base of the safe and down into the floor. I confirmed my suspicions of a vertical entrance by a close inspection of the maw.

I bent double to place my head within the safe, directly above the hole, and shone my electric torch down this passage. What I saw was an empty, narrow vertical tunnel with archaic metal rungs set into equally antiquated brickwork. With this prudent assessment, I also observed a floor below. Mr. Smith had perhaps left his home via that passage for some reason and, through trickery or aid, sealed the entrance to the vault below his home after passing through it. I thought only of my correspondence with him and knew that I had to find him, for there would be a very good reason why he was down there. Even at that point, I naively imagined that he had befallen some minor incident below, and was unable to return. So I chose to explore this vertical entrance to unknown depths, even if only briefly, and rescue him. I switched on my electric torch and positioned myself as to slide backwards into the safe. My feet easily found the rungs, and I descended.

ii.

After the short climb down the rungs, I reached the bottom of the ladder and turned to observe my surroundings. I could discern that the wall's age was far greater than the house above. In front of me, a passage sloped downward a little way and then broke into steps, their build equally archaic; worn shallows in the centre of the stairs almost made them a steep slope. I walked down into the darkness with the beam of my electric torch seeking a way ahead.

I lost count of the turns I made and the hours I spent walking downwards; the stairs only constancy was a decline, but they writhed, tilted, and spiralled at times to angles so steep I found it hard to traverse them without falling. To make this clear is of the utmost importance to me: there were no other passages crossing the path of the one I traversed, and there was no indication of sealed doorways.

While I was proceeding downward and about to give up, for I was convinced that this passage was endless, the most curious panic crossed my mind. I believed that I could hear something from higher up the staircase, distant and quite remote. At times I rushed, as behind me the scraping of walls and stairs echoed closer, and it was extremely unpleasant to hear. I shudder to recall the idea of some bulky body forcing its way toward my position with such speed it pulled at the

143

bricks. Clearly someone had followed my entrance into this stairwell and now sought me out. I often waited in silence as not to let my feet intertwine with the noises I was hearing. Whatever did bear down on me from the secret entrance, I could not make out anything definite. It was with such in mind, I sped up my descent to the location of Mr. Smith and to safety.

As I finally reached the last stair, a brick archway led into a stone chamber. I swept my electric torch about and noticed that the architecture in the room had changed to large grey blocks of stone, though this room did not appear to be an original vestibule. The brickwork about the entrance arch looked far too penetrative to be constructed at the same time as the stonework. The stairwell of which I had traversed was ancient in its build, yet this new chamber held the look of aeons past. I calculated that I must have been travelling for two hours by the time I got to the chamber where I finished my descent. After a brief glance at my pocket watch, I had clearly misjudged the elapse of time, for only a mere fifteen minutes had passed.

There was a second arch at the other end of the room. As I passed the boundary into the next space, what I saw was a wider passageway leading left and right. It had such a strange angle of its building; the whole corridor was at a *slant* to the right. Within the chamber before it, I had not noticed this offset, for everything was squared with the obtuse degree.

I then attempted to distract myself with the sweep of my electric torch as the numb feeling of being followed returned, though I could not tell whether the source was emanating from in front of or behind me. As I looked into this hall, I took note that other arches, similar to the one I just exited, were spaced in both directions along the far wall. The hall was then divided centrally with great stone pillars that ascended into the darkness, for not even my electric torch would reveal their apex. Apparent on these pronounced monolithic pillars were iron brackets clearly designed for torches, though all of them I observed from the doorway were empty.

The stolid angle of the floor inclined me to travel right; of which I gladly did. I began walking, when ahead I noticed a white shape on the floor to the side of a doorway. The illumination of my electric light revealed it to be an envelope, and, once I had closed in, I was sickened to see upon retrieval that it was addressed with the familiar hand of Mr. Smith. I would say his hand should have been comforting in the lonely darkness, but it only filled me with a dread that my presence here was somehow planned. A creeping and terrible thought of this letter being the trigger for some ambush swept over my mind, making me push myself into the freezing corner between the wall and a colossal arch, hiding myself from the antechamber through which I had entered the hall.

Yet, I did not switch off my electric torch to hide from any potential ambusher. Instead, I kept the light on and swung it about, flashing its beam from distant doorway to arch and back. What I heard then came from behind me, around the corner, though I did not dare to glance back. I positioned the beam of my torch down to the floor and listened intently. From the antechamber through which I had entered this hall, I heard a scraping as something hauled its bulk through the brick arch and into the room. The sound it made was beyond any accurate description; a dripping and gulping far more watery than any human voice could produce. A slapping of something wet upon stone followed this vomiting of sounds, but it then stopped at once, arrested for some reason. I waited for such a time listening; I judge it must have been an hour of silence before I calmed somewhat.

I still clutched the letter I had picked up and only then I opened it, for little else was letting me keep a grasp upon my nerves.

November 9th
I know I must tell you this all right away, for I do not know what esoteric order constructed this monstrosity. Such horror should never be uncovered and left to the world! It taunts me with sounds since its discovery, it provokes those things *in the pits; making them cry and moan, and yet never feeding them. What I could never imagine is the*

The next sentence was torn through the centre, with the rest of the letter absent from the envelope. I had never observed Mr. Smith to write this way, yet it was unmistakably in his hand. I sat and read the lines repeatedly until I could recall them on demand. They soothed me further as the familiar rounding of the letters reminded me of happier communications.

I certainly wasn't sure any longer if anything was behind me, still in the exit chamber, but I knew that I could not bring myself to leave that way and would have to carry on and find another flight of stairs and hopefully Mr. Smith too, for he clearly passed this way today. I slid along the wall, and, when I was at a more comfortable distance, I ran a little way and stopped.

iii.

I stood and swept the torch beam down the passage. As I now walked, I passed many gaping identical doorways into black chambers. I hesitantly investigated some and found most empty, but others contained absolutely rotten packing crates; their date and age were impossible to judge. They were stacked in the rooms and had been afflicted by a terrifying decomposition that made both the wood and nails sag with organic absurdity. All of the crates I dared looked within were empty and no remains or residue gave insight as to their original use.

One room I passed suddenly assaulted me with the reek of a terrifyingly recognizable and foetid air. It was not the smell itself; it was the damned *familiarity* of it which made me gag. I instinctively backed away to the other side of the hall and shone my electric torch cautiously toward the distant threshold. I saw the desiccated remains of some animal's leg lying across the doorway. The bones were clearly visible but yellowed horribly. My head swam as I flicked away the beam and caught sight of the cell's far wall. For a moment, a flicker and nothing more, I am sure that I saw a *heap* of skulls, and not all animal skulls either, all stacked within. I let the light linger to the side of the door, not allowing myself to turn the electric torch back into that room. Even though the familiar stench battered me, I edged away never wanting to truly see what was against the far wall or take a step closer than necessary.

I felt the need to escape down the skewed stone hall and away from the room, pushing me further away from the exit I knew of. I noticed also with great alarm that I could hardly grip the Bakelite case of my electric torch, for a terrible tremor had set into my limbs, which I did my utmost to control.

iv.

The hallway continued a great distance before an intersection pierced the sides at such an angle that the slanted floor upon which I travelled twisted up at the right hand side with a perplexing gradient to align itself with the intersecting tunnel. I stopped short as the floor began its gradual banking. I felt nothing but complete disorientation as the floor changed in this way. The damnedest thing was that this banking gave the impression that I was not meant to even be using this passage. I don't understand how a person would have progressed further down this hallway without great difficulty.

At that moment, the shaking in my hands grew with such ferocity that I turned and walked to the archways that lined the hall to rest my arm upon it for support. The very moment I placed my hand upon the freezing stone to hang my head, I heard behind me a sluggish form of locomotion that abruptly ceased. My footsteps and breathing had previously masked its faint sound of pursuit. There was a draw of breath, bubbling through a fluid. As I stood frozen with fright, I could not turn my head to look back up the sloping hallway.

There was a silence for a time, which enabled me to draw myself up against the wall. With such sluggishness of motion, I finally looked back the way I had come for an indication of what had made the sounds. Absolute pitch blackness looked back at me, as silent as before. As I finally exhaled, there was a shuffling; *something* clicked against the stone in the middle distance as it moved.

It was then, for the first time, the panic caused me to drop my electric torch with a loud clatter upon the floor and crack the casing. As the electric torch revolved toward the left-hand wall, it flashed into the antechamber directly across the corridor. It flashed so quickly into that room that I did not see the whole thing in detail, but, being frozen with a terror, all I recall seeing was a door on the far inside wall. The slurping and clicking in the dark retreated from the strike of my electric torch upon the stone floor and faded away as the noise travelled up the corridor's slope. I was beset upon again by foetid air, the cursed and identifiable odour I smelt upon opening the secret entrance and the same air from the room with animal remains across the door. Its horrid familiarity had not lost any impact upon me, and it came in an almighty gust, as if an exhalation of putrid breath whispered past me.

Though in utter panic, I managed to pull myself around the pillar and cower between the bitter wall and arch monolith. Here was the place where my electric torch had come to rest and pointed light across the hall.

I sat for a time; waiting in the silence of the hall. I thought I was there for two hours steadying myself, though it was only after that period that I looked at my pocket watch and noticed the time. I realised then my error, only twenty minutes had passed. After this discovery I came to my senses; the sound I heard must have been someone in pursuit of me all the way from the vault entrance. I had the unerring sensation that they meant to do me harm, so I was right to avoid them.

I boldly tried to stand, but, such stiffness had settled into my bones, I had to rub my legs with vigour to awake the circulation. As I finally stood, I picked up my electric torch. By mistake I spilled a faint trail of torchlight into the doorway of the opposite chamber, and I remembered the wooden door I had seen during my panic. I leant forward a little, squinting to bring clearer into focus the chamber's interior. I could make out very little, so I locked my vision onto the archway leading into the chamber and boldly strode across the hall. As I made it into the chamber, I began to sweep my light about the room.

The door I had seen was fastened shut, locked with little indication as to how it was sealed. As I had not seen a gated entrance at all during my time within the vault, I had to assume that this perhaps led to a significant room or even to an exit. I studied the closed portal in detail with my light, and, at one point, I stood back to think upon how I might go about opening it, and, suddenly, I heard a tapping coming through the decaying wood. It startled me such that I stumbled over backwards, landing hard upon the stone. A horrid creeping sensation washed over me as I stared up at the door looming over me. Again, then came a rapping, harder still this time.

I was frozen in place, my voice locked as well as my limbs. The only thing breaking my paralysation was a shaking in my body that pinned me to the floor in horrid silence. Moments later, I then heard a desperate weeping drift through the timber-sealed entrance. I gained a little courage in this very muffled, yet human, sound and managed to right myself. Once again, deathly silence took hold and lasted for such a time I began to think I might have heard the sounds from another source.

What wracked me with blind fear was stillness being pierced by an almighty wail combined with ferocious slamming upon the door. So violent was this battering that it shook the timber construction upon its hinges. With its fierce and unexpected start, the hammering was arrested instantaneously. So sharp was its cut-off that I was almost as stunned with the abrupt plunge back into dreadful silence. I was rooted to the spot as my mind spun. Perhaps what had happened to me had also happened to Mr. Smith, and, so, I was quickly convinced that he had made his way into the room beyond, looking for an exit to this foul place, and was imprisoned as the door closed itself. The cry of desperation was obviously caused by his state of panic at being trapped. I took to studying the door with great care, for I thought some method must unlock it, since it did not have a keyhole.

I finally spotted a metal bar that was imbedded into the stone and gave it a push. There was a rolling sound within the door, and I observed the barrier shift a fraction upon its hinges into the adjoined room. I gave the timber door a steady thrust with my shoulder, and it swung inward.

v.

As I stepped through, the difference in architecture was immediate, so I pushed the entrance partially closed, being mindful to drive a loose rock between the doorjamb and the door. I then edged away from the pitch-black horizontal slot that the door and frame now made. I swallowed hard, looked at my pocket watch, and realised how long it must have taken to find the locking mechanism. I feared that Mr. Smith must have lost hope and moved on to elsewhere, perhaps to another location in search of an exit.

I swung the torch beam about in hope of seeing him and saw that the room was incomplete. The floor was gritty and rough, with a few slabs placed at intervals with no care paid towards their setting. The chamber's bare earth floor was awash with rubble, singularly punctuated with an open pit steeped in shadows. It was some attempt to shape the room into an identical version of the previous chamber, with the exception being its length and apparent unfinished well.

Towards the far end of the long room, I could just make out a wide arch. I started towards it, only for my light to show that a back wall was close after this arched threshold. This made the annex a simple square room with equally roughened features of construction. As I tentatively passed the pit that brimmed with pitch shadows, I reached the entrance to this adjoined space. Then abruptly I heard a recognizable noise behind me, and I spun with the light closing dimly upon the far door. The sound was of hinges moving under the weight of the door's weighty construction. The slot of pitch-blackness was wider now; I could clearly see that the vertical gap between the door and the frame had widened, not closed. The door now stood half open rather than ajar.

I did not move for some time. I looked to that door and listened for other sounds that held any ghastly familiarity. My mind was bending; I could feel the creeping sensation return, something *was* looking at me from across the room. I backed away further into the annex and came into contact with a wooden construction that I had not noticed before. I had missed it previously as the narrow frame was obscured by a jut of rock from the archway. I glanced up and saw that this chamber was actually a shaft up into darkness, the tall timber frame stood within the shaft. Attached to the wooden tower was a ladder ascending into the gloom. The structure as a whole was somewhat dilapidated and looked immensely old. The wood was coloured a mix of grey and green and dusty to the touch.

I quickly switched my sight back and forth from the door down the end of the room to the wooden scaffolding, for something between the timbers had caught my eye. There was a shape unpleasantly memorable in its outline within the slats. A sackcloth sheet stained with dark round patterns lay over a chair-shaped object, except the top of the covered item, which looked moderately spherical and tilted forward. Its outline was the most petrifying thing I had seen, as I suddenly guessed to whom this shape could belong.

Unexpectedly the cloth then twitched with what seemed to be its own volition and fell away from the body it covered.

I do not remember much at this point except my head striking the stone floor, for I was wholly overcome and fainted. My torch then left my grasp, and I let out a murmur of frustration, as I tried to follow the torchlight's erratic rolling and jumping back towards the heavy entrance through which I had passed.

At some point in my blurry-eyed, sickening stumble after the increasing velocity that electric torch travelled, it suddenly lurched and disappeared into the black pit further down the room. I made it to the edge of this well only to see my torch in a clattering descent, finishing in a sudden thud that killed any illumination that reached up from the fissure. I was plunged into absolute pitch-blackness. The most horrifying thing was what reached up from the shaft into my ears.

I made out a moaning, a long-winded lament of pitiful gurgling.

The words of Mr. Smith's letter came back to my mind with such poignancy I cried out with a feeble whine. Such ghastly things filled my mind; I was sightless in the black of a freezing stone hell. I started to crawl back to the ladder, thinking only of ascent, knowing that the ground above my head was the only place I should be, not within the evil of this stone monstrosity.

Crawling in the darkness, I felt the floor move beneath me. I felt it tilt upward and to angles that made me slide about as I desperately grasped for some means of stopping myself from moving in this unwanted and unnatural way. Disorientated, I scrabbled my way across the floor in panic; seeking anything of familiarity, I once happened upon the hole that still had revolting noises emanating from it. I fought unconsciousness with all my might as deathly terror flooded over me. With backing away, I tried to work out the position of the ladder, so I then turned and headed in the blackness toward its position.

With great alarm I was not met with ice-cold rungs, but the feel of sackcloth in my outstretched hand. I screamed, turning back immediately.

I clambered away, with my uncovered hands becoming quite painful because of the constant contact with the ground. In my panic, I entertained the thought of attempting to stand. At that very second, the floor moved again to such an angle I skidded with a yelp and struck a wall. I was lucky not to strike my head upon a jut of rock that would have rendered me unconscious. With a new dread-filled resolve, I became aware of my own rapid breathing, and I made a move, crawling, back towards where I thought the ladder might be.

I was in the depths of unexplainable fear. I had lost my electric torch to a gurgling pit, which I encountered twice due to the ghastly tilting of the room. As my mind reeled from fears that assaulted my final crux of bravery, I cried out with such weakness and gibbering in an attempt to ward off anything close by, my own voice became broken and alien to me.

The thing under the sackcloth filled my thoughts as I moved. Was the search for Mr. Smith now complete? I believe I had found him in a state I could scarcely imagine or come to accept; yet it was not the body's stage of decomposition that terrified me so. What I saw was a face of a man that held an expression of exceptional familiarity, but it was so twisted and contorted in agony.

I crawled and cried for anyone to help me escape the horrors that lurked about me. The remaining hours of my ordeal were spent in this state, as I searched for a solution. Then, at the ends of my searching fingers I felt a cold, dusty hardness, and the sharp point of a nail. I had finally managed to reach the timber construction within the arched annex. I carefully searched around its base for the ladder, so very carefully as not to touch the sackcloth that was close by.

The whole desperate search for the ladder was utterly horrid. I knew that next to me Mr. Smith's expression stared at me through the slats with bloated eyes and swollen maw. It was only then that I found the first rung upon which I pulled myself up and grasped for the next.

I urged myself upward with simple mutterings of reassurance. I needed there to be an egress at the top of the tower, so that I could fling it wide and bolt into the night. Somehow, even the most pitch-black nights in the city did not compare to the darkness I was experiencing. The climb seemed to be endless, though I did not stop even when my muscles were wracked with pain and fatigue. However much I willed there to be an exit, when I finally reached the top of the ladder, I found a platform atop the tower with no further avenue of escape.

I lay prone on the tower's dais attempting to gain control of my frantic breathing. I turned around to the ladder's top and looked down in some vain hope that I might see something from this elevation. I could not tell if my eyes were deceiving me at first, but slowly I witnessed a light within the room below grow into a dull, ill-looking aura. It poured through the annex's arch and lit the floor. Then I felt a small shudder in the tower as below something hit against its slats.

I did not observe anything close by that could cause such a shake, but I gasped in horror as I realised that it must have come from *inside* the slats. Then, a slight scraping vibration reached my fingers from below, and I saw upon the tower's side distinctly human-shaped shoulders and head emerge from the gap in the boards. A stabbing, bizarre fear awoke inside me as the body slid through the creaking slats, arms wheeling, and slumped onto the floor, next to the tower. I clawed desperately at the wooden boards, unable to stop my alarm or find a solution to this inevitable demise at the hands of a bloated, wrenched corpse. My eyes were locked onto the movement below; when just as suddenly, I made an audible noise, and the light died, and I was plunged back into darkness. After a minute had passed, I felt the platform vibrate.

With my panic at fever pitch, I tried to back away, but found only the edges of the platform. Then, again came the shudder of the timbers, and below me the frame creaked. I held tightly onto the dusty timbers, and a regular shudder grew, making the frame protest and creek beneath me. In the pitch-blackness, I heard a plank loosen from its nails and splinter onto the floor below. Yet, there was suddenly another source of light; the tiniest of chinks flashed a pinhead of light into my eyes as I hung onto the edges of the dais. My will was then totally bent upon it, and I reached out, finding a wall was quite close. My clawing hands dug at the source as in my blindness I felt a flat stone sill with a thick wooden board blocking a hole. I dug my nails into the wood and pulled at every purchase point I could find. I was weeping, scratching at the chink of light, desperate to increase its size.

Behind me the shuddering stopped, and I heard a distant striking of metal, a regular sound of hard, deliberate feet ascending the metal rungs of the ladder. I flung myself against the wooden board again and again, with the horrifying noises from below ever rising.

There was an almighty cracking, and my shoulder was torn with pain, yet the board upon which I was hammering broke. In my panicked rush, blinded by the new light that rushed in, I attempted to haul myself through the opening. I knew that in doing so I had severely injured myself, but the flood of relief was starting to become palpable as I managed to get my head and arms through the small arch. Now blind with blurry light and dust in my eyes, I was spent with the effort of breaking the board, for I could not pull myself up and out through the exit.

As I scraped my feet against the inside wall and heaved my torso through the hole, I felt something deathly cold touch my leg. I knew it wasn't the stonework into which my feet dug, or the boards of the tower; I involuntarily screamed with such zeal I half deafened myself. With absolute haste I finally pulled my legs out of the pitch-black hole, and I rolled away across an unrecognisable cellar floor, weeping with fear.

The last thing I remember before passing out and the inevitable arrest for trespass was clearing my eyes somewhat and looking back towards the arched drain through which I had come. Despite my battered state, I know that I saw the face of Mr. Artemas Smith grinning back at me, his life restored, looking just the same as the picture I had been given. Except, as his face retreated from the light, his eyes took on a sickly hue, and his skin peeled away from his face. That horrid grin was now a snarl of hunger unsatisfied, one which will haunt me forever.

The Fall of the Old Faith

Ed Martin

The narrative I set down before you is written on the advice of my psychiatrist, one Dr. Daniel Wolger. It is with his help that I have attempted to piece together the events of the early hours of 28th April 1997; I present them to you, my reader, not in the expectation of being believed, but in the hope that the act of articulating my experiences will assist my recovery and restore some peace to my senses. Let it suffice for the moment to say that on the night in question I underwent an experience, the details of which I must recount with care: to say it began with a mere sound might be true in the literal sense, but, I fear, horribly misleading.

If the end of my tale is by necessity imprecise, I hope that the clarity with which I remember its beginning may serve as some small compensation. I can tell you with no little confidence that it began at around half past five on the evening of 23rd April. I was walking through the woods that spot Thrushmore Common in Surrey on my way home from work. Although something of a detour from the college, the bluebells that grow up in the woods of the common make it a pleasant place for a stroll on a warm evening in mid spring, and a lengthy diversion through the area is by no means unusual for me at this time of year. Over time I have come to know the place intimately, a fact that made the event I am about to set down in writing for the first time all the more unusual and incomprehensible.

I had misjudged the weather that day; the clouds that had been only threatening the horizon as I had entered the wood were now looming grimly overhead as I passed the thickest and densest patch of trees. What little sky was visible under the canopy was veiled (I remember thinking at the time that it seemed odd for clouds so distant to approach so quickly). The wind was beginning to pick up, and spots of rain on the breeze carried the promise of a heavy storm, for which I was entirely unprepared. It then happened, as I was pulling my jacket closer around myself and making for home at speed, that I heard the noise that would precipitate this entire strange affair.

It was the sound of a door opening. Large and heavy, opening slowly. I can remember looking around suddenly, startled by such an incongruous noise. As a moment passed, however, my initial start came to be replaced with a different sense, one that might perhaps be considered eager curiosity. Without having heard the noise yourself, you may consider it strange that I should have become so enraptured rather than dismiss the noise as a mere trick of the woods. After all, the wind was blowing, the branches above me curling and colliding as if locked in applause. There must surely have been a thousand entirely logical explanations for what I heard — always assuming, of course, that I did not merely imagine the entire affair. That, of course, was entirely plausible, my dark and gloomy surroundings providing a more than ample backdrop for a flight of fancy. I must confess that this rational way of thinking did indeed occur to me at the time; yet, for some reason that I could not have explained, I felt compelled to remain a moment.

Perhaps unsurprisingly, my cursory search of the area yielded nothing of note. In the gathering gloom, the distorting shadows of the trees gave the wood a sinister, living presence; yet neither the branches above me nor the ferns at my ankles gave me the least reason to suspect that anything might be amiss. However, the more my search proved fruitless, the more intense my sense of curiosity grew as it became ever clearer that there was nothing around that could possibly have accounted for the sound of an opening door.

The branches in the canopy, heavy though they looked, were thrashing far too feverishly to have caused the slow, deliberate creak I had heard. No, what I heard was a door opening. There could be no doubt. Yet this observation was objectively absurd, made as it was by a man standing in dense woodland, no fewer than two miles from the nearest building. This contradiction only served to further whet my desire to resolve the mystery.

Eventually, the coming rain began to patter over the leaves above me, and I was forced to abandon the search, if not the train of thought; I made the rest of the journey home at a fair jog, but could not avoid a thorough soaking. As I sat in my living room, drying off and replaying the memory of the sound in my head, a thought occurred to me that may well have unnerved me into moving earlier, had it struck me in the woods: the sound, such as it was, stood out by way of having one particularly disturbing characteristic, not shared by any other noise from the empty woodland. It had been, simply and plainly, *deliberate*. Try as I might, I could not possibly put this thought out of my head. I found myself, credulous as it may seem, resolving to continue my investigation at the earliest opportunity. There was, after all, the possibility that some old structure did exist somewhere in the woods without my knowing. Such things are not unheard of.

In retrospect, I should perhaps have dwelt rather more upon the unnatural sense of compulsion I felt to investigate the mystery. I am not by nature a gullible man, and, under normal circumstances, it may not have occurred to me that a study of local history would be an appropriate course of action. As it was, I regrettably neglected to question my state of mind and instead threw myself into my studies, which began the next morning at Thrushmore Library.

◆

As the automatic doors of the front entrance swished shut behind me, I was forced to admit to myself that I had absolutely no idea where to begin my search. I felt the eyes of an elderly librarian on me as I stood ineptly in the lobby, scanning the signs over nearby shelves. Acutely aware of how little real evidence I had on which to base my investigations, and keen to avoid wasting my own time, I tentatively made my way across the space and approached the librarian. Despite myself, I felt the hot sting of self-consciousness as I realised that she had been subtly observing me since my arrival.

"How may I help you, sir?" she enquired politely, her somewhat cracked voice never rising above the gentlest murmur. I replied, without elaboration, that I was looking to research some features of the area and hoped she could oblige me by pointing out the library's local history section, should it have one. With the clipped efficiency that one sometimes sees in the elderly, she led me from the desk and pointed me towards a shadowy corner of the room containing the general history and geography sections. I was hardly surprised to find the local history section to be very small, consisting only of a single shelf, on which several gaps between the books were visible.

"We don't see many people wanting to research the area," noted the lady softly, as I set my belongings on the nearest desk.

"Oh?" I replied, with mild surprise. "It looks to me like there are several books out at the moment."

"I'm afraid some volumes have gone missing recently."

I stopped, my curiosity engaged. "Really? Any important ones?"

The lady eyed me with barely-concealed wariness. Inwardly, I regretted showing so much interest so openly.

"I'd hardly have said there were many important books here to begin with," she said with measured control. "There aren't many that stick in my mind. I do recall one rather lovely hardback on the architecture of the village. That'll be hard to replace. Aside from that I'm not sure I know what you're referring to. I suppose whether or not a book is significant would depend on what you're looking for?" This last remark was unmistakeably quizzical in tone.

"A layman's interest," I replied quickly, conscious of the truth of that remark. It occurred to me that a book on architecture would have been exactly the starting point I needed. The coincidence of it, that the little librarian should single that text out, swam uneasily in my mind for a moment. "One of those cases where you only find out what you're looking for when you find it," I added.

"Indeed. Is there anything else I can help you with?"

"No, thank you. You've been very helpful."

"I'll be at the main desk if you need anything, then."

I thanked her again as she shuffled off. I scanned the shelf, hoping that one of the titles in front of me would present itself as potentially fruitful. All the while, I felt the librarian's gaze at my back.

Rapidly, I began to understand what she had meant when she had told me that there was little of significance. Most of the books on the shelf were turgid and inconsequential volumes on subjects such as the history of wheat-milling in the area and an obscure artistic movement, one minor associate of which had once lived nearby. I did recognise one author, Dr. Reginald Lowe, as a local historian of antiquarian interests, but his solitary book seemed irrelevant. Idly my hand passed from one volume to another, and I began to find the idea of coming to this library at all a mistake. What, after all, was I really looking for? Where was I expecting to find it? I could have read every book on the shelf and still come away with nothing useful. However, as I was beginning to think to myself that I should quit my endeavour altogether, my hand fell upon a small, slim pamphlet that I had failed to notice the first several times I had looked over the shelf. I found my hand gravitating towards it, and was overcome with the inexplicable feeling that I had found something of worth at last. Compelled by my own curiosity, I picked the tiny volume up and returned with it to my desk, noticing as I did so its title:

DEFECTIO RELIGIAE ANTIQUA

I found no publication date and it was impossible to guess how old it was: it was in reasonable condition, but something in its presentation suggested age. It was bound with thread, rather than the modern staples I might suppose for a publication of its size, and seemed to imitate the typeset printing of centuries past. (It would not strike me as suspicious until later that the pamphlet had no return sheet or printed code, or anything else to explicitly mark it as property of the library). The details of the text, impenetrably written in an archaic style, were lurid and, to my mind, improbable to say the least. They concerned what we might today call a witch cult, who were — it said — well established in the area up until the Reformation. The text contained many sordid stories of blood sacrifice and sexual deviance of the sort that might be expected from a religious tract, the original writing of which may even have been contemporaneous with the events it described. It put me in mind, as a point of reference, with the gruesome stories told of the extinct Knights Templar at the hands of the Inquisition.

I took some small pleasure in the details, thinking them amusing spooky tales, but never seriously considered them useful or genuinely informative. Once again I found myself at a dead end. However, turning to the final pages, I found a reference to something altogether more interesting; I swiftly thought to look around me — seeing that the librarian appeared now to be absorbed in conversation with another visitor — before returning to the text. The pamphlet alleged that a chapel belonging to this unnamed group had survived well into the seventeenth century, hidden from prying eyes in the deep woods of what is now Thrushmore Common. Included on the final page was what looked like a rough woodcut of the supposed chapel's interior. As far as I could tell, the chapel would be a small affair of a single interior space, enough to comfortably fit perhaps twenty people plus an altar. Otherwise, the details were unclear, and I was hesitant to infer too much.

As I was leaving, the librarian looked up from her desk to catch my eye.

"Did you find what you were looking for in the end?"

"No, unfortunately," I lied. "I wasn't really expecting to, if I'm honest. Goodbye."

"Have a good day, sir."

The pamphlet sat snugly in my inside jacket pocket. I had decided that, with nothing to indicate its being the property of the library, its absence was unlikely to be noticed. You will no doubt remark on my foolishness; I, regrettably, did not.

♦

Two days later I returned to the wood. It was the weekend by this point, and the countryside was thick with ramblers and dog walkers, to whom I should not have liked to explain myself. I cast a glimpse at the fields around me as I stole into the deeper woodland where I had first heard the sound of the door and experienced the strange, compelling sensation that drew me into my investigations. Fortunately, despite the presence of a few walkers, I did not see anybody looking in my direction and was able to disappear into the thickets. To my considerable annoyance it appeared as if the sky was darkening again, despite the weather forecast suggesting nothing but glorious sunshine all day. It had certainly seemed glorious when I left home. At the time I was more irritated about leaving my umbrella behind; in retrospect the unnatural speed of the clouds, which drew over me like a stage curtain, should perhaps have caught my attention rather more than they did. It was almost as if the wood and I were being hidden from the rest of the world, the better for it to reveal the secret at its heart.

The walk gave me time to think my investigations through. There had to be, I reasoned, some piece of physical evidence remaining on the site, however small. The fact of my hearing the noise, and then discovering the text in the library, seemed too much of a coincidence to put down to my imagination. The building in question was supposedly a small one, which could perhaps account for the absence of any apparent ruins waiting to be discovered by one of the innumerable people who must have walked through the site over the centuries. Had the building been made of stone, it was more than plausible that its masonry may have been taken, a piece at a time, for other uses. Therefore, if anything were to survive, it would probably be the foundation stones, hidden from disturbance by the thick carpet of ferns and bracken that covered the area. For this reason I had thought to stow some thick gardening gloves in my rucksack before setting out.

I arrived at the site at around three o' clock in the afternoon. The wind had become unsettlingly cold and, while no rain was falling yet, the sky was heavy and dark. I pulled my coat around myself, donned the gloves, and paused for a moment, wondering where to start. I was, as you may be supposing, on a fool's errand. I could hardly wrench up every fern in the clearing, after all, and my expectations were still nothing but pure speculation. Nonetheless I remained compelled to stay and, after finding the spot where I had been standing when I heard the noise, decided to begin walking round the area in rough circles, sweeping my feet before me with each step, hoping that I might eventually discover something beneath the foliage. A crude and ineffectual method of surveying this was, and you would be perfectly right to tell me that my chances of any meaningful success would be too slim to make the effort worthwhile. How naïve of me, therefore, not to take note of the extreme unlikelihood of my foot striking what felt like a large flat stone, some twenty minutes after beginning.

Immediately, I reached down and wrenched aside the greenery. I saw, just as I had suspected, a heavily-worn stone jutting at a slight angle out of the ground. It was the remains of a foundation, I was sure. Despite its age and heavy wear — no doubt the ground must have slightly subsided at some point in the past — it retained its flattened appearance, which betrayed the work of a craftsman's hands. It was all I could do to keep from laughing. At last, I had found definitive proof that a building had stood on this site at some point in the past. Of course it remained to be seen exactly what this building had been (not to mention whether it corresponded with the sordid little pamphlet's allegations), but, nevertheless, it vindicated my efforts.

After photographing the stone from various angles and with my foot deliberately in shot for the purposes of scale, my first thought was to return home. The sky did seem very threatening and, frankly, I had been lucky to get this far without a second soaking. It occurred to me after a moment though that, the building being small, the chance of my locating the other three stones was now better than before. The second stone was unlikely to be more than twenty yards away in any direction and a handful of criss-crossing paths around the area, where the bare ground was exposed, helped narrow down the possibilities. So it was that the second stone was unearthed within a few minutes (the choice of angle helped by an educated guess that the path leading to the site may once have led to its doors).

Having found two stones, I could hardly abandon the search for the other two, rain be damned. Arbitrarily I picked a direction at ninety degrees to the former, but several minutes of kicking through the undergrowth yielded nothing. I tried the other direction, but my search proved similarly fruitless. Eventually the stone was found by my returning to the rough circular pattern of before; the third stone, it turned out, was not located on the perpendicular but at an angle slightly above it. The conclusion this suggested — simple as it seems — had quite honestly never occurred to me: this building, in its rough and crude way, may have had five sides instead of four, presumably arranged in the shape of a pentagon. Following this hunch, two more stones were located in their expected places to confirm the hypothesis.

I decided to retrace the pentagonal layout of the stones one final time, taking photographs for every one, before setting off home (astoundingly, I still remained dry). At the fifth and final stone, reaching down to gather my rucksack, I was suddenly overcome by the most peculiar sense of anxiety. It was the feeling a person might get when they realise that they are responsible for some negligence or offence; the inescapable certainty that they have done some wrong and must be punished for it. I attempted to dismiss this as silliness, or possibly overexcitement at my discovery, but nevertheless gathered my belongings more slowly and cautiously than I might otherwise have done. I also took greater pains to look around me before I left for home.

It was at the final turn towards the path home that I suddenly jumped at the sight of something moving soundlessly behind a tree, out of the corner of my left eye. I spun around, thinking to have been discovered by someone, and darted towards the movement. Reaching the tree, however, I found nothing behind it and supposed that I had been mistaken. No sooner had I reassured myself thus but another figure sidled into the darkness of the wood, some yards ahead of me. In the growing darkness, I was unable to see it clearly, but its presence was undeniable. Some form, some indeterminate black shape, had noiselessly glided out of sight. I confess my will to investigate this new mystery drained from me; in fact, I was so overcome with nerves that I turned to go at a sprint, barely slowing until I had reached the edge of the woods again. I did not look behind me, and I hope I need not defend myself on this point to a sympathetic reader.

I settled my nerves at home with a strong brandy. With time and quiet, my earlier fears left me and the excitement of my discovery returned. I had unearthed definitive proof of a new and hitherto undiscovered archaeological site; the implications were profound. To that end, it was immediately apparent that I had unfortunately come as far as I could purely on my own initiative. I would require, I knew, professional support.

At this moment the name of Reginald Lowe occurred to me, and I remembered where I had seen it before: in the library, shortly before I had found the pamphlet. He was, if I remembered correctly, a local historian and antiquarian: he sounded like the best person to get in touch with. Luckily, he retained a reasonable profile from some of the minor books of history that he had published some years back, and it was the work of a few moments to send him an email summarising my discovery of the pamphlet. I omitted all mention, of course, of the strange sights and noises that had accompanied me. News of the building, I decided, could wait until I knew more about the man.

Despite the lateness of the hour, I was not kept waiting long for a reply. I was struck by its brusque tone:

Dear Sir,

Please call tomorrow (Sunday) if available. I am free after 10.30 a.m. Please bring the pamphlet with you, assuming nothing has happened to it.
I look forward to meeting you.

Yours,
Reginald Lowe (Dr)

I went to bed that night still puzzling over his mention of the pamphlet, which was sitting quite safely on my bedside table. Whatever did he mean, "assuming nothing has happened to it"? What reason did he have to suggest that I might have lost it? I resolved to ask him about this in the morning.

Incidentally, I recall being woken during the night by the sound of a police car outside, with its lights shining through my curtains; I dozed back off to sleep to the sound of the lady in the flat below being calmed by two officers. I found out the next morning that she believed she had seen an intruder in the garden, but, when asked, had been unable to provide a clear description.

◆

It was around eleven o' clock the next morning that I knocked on Dr. Lowe's door. His strange suggestion of the loss of the pamphlet was still in my mind; despite myself, I had taken care on the journey over to pat my pocket on several occasions to check its presence. I was kept waiting at the door for some moments before the old historian finally shuffled his way over.

"You must be the young man with the pamphlet," he said, by way of a greeting.

The politeness of my own greeting was not returned. The old man merely gestured for me to enter behind him, leading me to a cluttered sitting room. He walked slowly, with a slight hobble, and I found myself trying to guess his age. As he busied himself making an unsolicited cup of tea, I took the liberty of observing my surroundings. Here was a man, I concluded, to whom work was the primary concern (social protocol coming a distant second). Every wall, as well as virtually every flat surface in the room, was covered with books: some new, many old, and all that I could see on the subject of history, archaeology, or folklore. Just as he was returning with the tea, my eye chanced upon the words *RELIGIAE ANTIQUA* written on the spine of a small book on a high shelf. It did not appear to have, at first glance, an author's credit.

"May I see it?" were the peculiar gentleman's first words to me after sitting down in what was obviously a much-loved and well-used armchair.

"Excuse me?"

"The pamphlet you mentioned. You did bring it?"

Lowe's single-mindedness was beginning to wear on my nerves now. I decided to seize the initiative for myself.

"If you don't mind my saying so," I began, reaching into my pocket, "you seem a bit agitated. Is everything all right?"

Lowe did not answer. His gaze remained fixed on the pamphlet, which I now held on my lap. My right hand remained tightly clasping it. "Dr. Lowe?"

Lowe, for the first time, seemed to listen to me.

"Oh, forgive me," he mumbled with an air of genuine contrition. "Yes, I suppose I am rather preoccupied. Thank you very much for bringing it. I know how difficult to acquire these things are."

"I must say it wasn't difficult in the least," I responded, noting a concerned change in Lowe's demeanour at these words. I continued, somewhat more cautiously. "I chanced upon it in the library. It was on a shelf of local history. I believe one of your own works was there."

"The local library?"

"Yes. You were unaware of it?"

The old historian now spoke in hushed, guarded tones. His eyes never left the pamphlet.

"I'm afraid I was, yes. How strange that it escaped my notice there, and how lucky of you to have come across it by accident. May I ask if you know what it is?"

"It seems to be a religious tract, as far as I can see," I answered. I decided there could be no harm in handing it over; the old man accepted it without speaking. I noticed him attempting to suppress a slight tremble in his hands. "Of course, you're the expert, Dr. Lowe."

"Please, Reginald."

"Of course. Anyway, it has a lot to say about a Satanic cult in the area. It mentions a building in the woods of Thrushmore Common."

"So it does," replied Lowe, without looking up. I noticed that he had turned to the text's last pages immediately upon receiving it. He did not speak for a minute. Looking at his face, I began to wonder if he was really as old as I had taken him for. Eventually, he murmured:

"You borrowed this?"

I squirmed in my seat.

"Not exactly."

Lowe looked up. "You stole it?"

"It wasn't marked as library property. From what I gather from you, it's probably not on their catalogue. Why? Is it valuable?"

"If you mean is it worth money, then no. But it does shed light on a few matters."

"Do you believe its allegations then?" Earlier, I might have asked that question with incredulity, or even perhaps scorn. Now, for whatever reason, I asked out of sincere interest.

"Oh, there was a cult," he said. "That's a matter of historical record."

"But the stories about them?"

"Perhaps," he answered with a shrug. "Some are more plausible than others. This building, for example…"

The memory of the foundation stones burned in my mind. I decided, with difficulty, not to mention them and see where Lowe's musings would take him.

"Yes?"

"There are references to a chapel or sanctum in the woods in a few different places. Strange references, sometimes, and not all of them consistent with each other, but enough to suggest that something did once exist. Obviously there's nothing there now, but then there are no references to any demolition either, accidental or otherwise. Eventually records just, you know, stop. The mid seventeenth century is the last clear reference to it. It's as if it — whatever it was — just wasn't there one day. I've never been able to verify much for sure, you understand."

I pressed on.

"And the cult?"

"A few of them found themselves in trouble with the law, but never many. Most of them just disappeared too. I suppose a few of them might have moved on, or died, or rejoined society here and there, but it's a bit like the building really. Again it's more that records just stop one day."

The conversation continued through most of the next hour, mostly concerning various small details of local pagan lore that need not be documented here. All of this meeting that is relevant to my narrative has been recorded, save for one small exchange at the front door as I was preparing to leave. I had thanked him for the tea, and allowed him to keep the pamphlet for the time being (against my better judgement, but he had rather insisted). He asked me a question that, at once, confirmed the suspicions that had been building for some time.

"Have you seen or heard anything?"

"I'm sorry?"

"Anything strange?"

"Such as?"

"I don't know, really. Anything unusual."

"No," I answered immediately, so as not to be seen having to think about the question. "I really don't know what you mean."

"For the best, probably," he responded with a sardonic nod. "All the same, I know it can be tempting, compelling even, but I'd leave well alone if I were you."

"Thank you for your concern," I responded with a faint touch of anger, "but like I say I really don't —"

"You have mud on your boots. Trust me. Leave well alone. I'll look after the pamphlet."

I moved off, shutting his garden gate behind me, cursing my oversight and playing the meeting over in my mind. Of course he had known more than he had said, but then so had I. The old man was clearly wily. But then, thinking about it more, perhaps he wasn't so old after all. There had been something strange about that from the very beginning. Not old: more like worn, as if he had suffered a recent illness.

◆

I know I should probably explain the thought process that led me to return to the site later that night. You must be expecting it — after all, I can hardly call Lowe's parting words bad advice. You can see that much for yourself. But in truth, I doubt that I can explain it. All I can tell you is that he was right when he said it was tempting. More than that, it was seductive: it was a mystery that had chosen me to solve it. I had a duty to myself not to abandon it now.

This rather self-serving line of reasoning played endlessly across my mind as I trudged through the woods of Thrushmore Common in the early hours of Monday morning. I had my pocket torch in my hand, but the night was clear, with the full moon bright behind the occasional break in the trees. It was, I noticed, the clearest it had been in all my visits.

I cannot say exactly when I returned to the site itself, for checking my watch was hardly the first thing on my mind. My eyes instead remained fixed on what was in front of me. There, in the middle of the clearing, precisely where the stones had marked it out, stood the little five-sided chapel. Plain granite, as far as I could see in the moonlight, and entirely featureless along its walls save for the heavy wooden door in front of me, towards which my path led. A pale light could be seen dancing in the crack of the door, suggestive of whatever horror lurked inside. I stood still, stupefied. I did nothing. Strange as it may seem now, I thought nothing.

I reacted instead to the movement in the corner of my vision but only to the extent of turning my torch — my legs, it seemed, were content to remain rooted — to the black shape now emerging from the trees to my right. A man, I should say, wearing dark robes and a hood to obscure his features, but who would have been taller than any man I had ever seen if not for his strange hunched posture. Hearing a noise at my shoulder, I turned to see another figure, identically clad, sliding from the thickets behind me. Like its companion, it too was unknowable beneath its robes, and it too stood and moved in a peculiar twisted manner, as if one leg was somehow horrifically misshapen. The loathsome, shambling figures moved clumsily, but silently and swiftly towards the chapel. If they had noticed me, they did not give any indication that my presence concerned them.

Now, looking around and with the moonlight clear, I could see a third figure appear from further in front of me, and then a fourth, a fifth. I saw no distinguishing features on any of them: their robes bore no designs and cloaked them from head to toe. All moved oddly, limping, and I could infer all manner of obscene deformities beneath their coverings. Five in total, lurching with nauseating efficiency towards the chapel. As far as I could tell, each was moving towards one of the five corners. The two nearest me took up positions some ten feet from their corners where they both stopped, gazing intently at the building, for some minutes. I began to consider moving, but some combination of horror and fascination compelled me to remain standing, waiting for action. This action came, eventually, with the figure to my left moving as if by some prearranged signal towards the door, towards which I was directly facing. I stood, helpless, listening to the harsh creak of the wood twisting on its hinges, bathing in the sickly light that now flooded my vision.

I have considered, at times, attempting to describe what was inside the chapel. No words in my vocabulary have ever really seemed to do it justice — I have never found a way of evoking its dimensions. Instead, I will attempt to describe what it would have seen, looking out its doorway, to gaze at me.

It would have seen a tiny figure of such little consequence as to barely be worth considering. A form of mere flesh, cringing and pathetic, beneath value, beneath trouble. Does it trouble you to know that you crush a snail underfoot? No? Then the analogy is sufficient, for "as flies to wanton boys are we to the Gods; / They kill us for their sport."

♦

What happened next I cannot tell you directly, for I only know what I have been told. I know that I was discovered, apparently cataleptic, later that morning in the woods by Dr. Reginald Lowe. When questioned, he told the authorities that he had followed me out of concern for my well-being; that we had spoken, that I had acted strangely and given him reason to worry. Not the whole truth, I fear, but since it protected both of us, I can hardly complain. I know also that, come daybreak, a cursory search was mounted of the area in which I had been found: nothing out of the ordinary was discovered, save for five flat stones buried in the ground, arranged in a pentagonal shape, near where I had been lying.

♦

There we find the conclusion to my narrative. I wish I could say I felt more of a sense of catharsis in writing it down, although no doubt my psychiatrist, Dr. Wolger, will find much in it of professional interest. I am grateful for his support, and I hope, given time, soon that I might be able to return home and continue my work. Dr. Wolger did suggest that writing this narrative down would go some way towards helping me to that end. In truth, I am not treated badly here, although I do appreciate the nurses pulling down the blinds on nights when the moon is out.

Biographies

Jesse Bullington is the critically acclaimed author of *The Sad Tale of the Brothers Grossbart*, *The Enterprise of Death*, and most recently, *The Folly of the World*. Riddled with grave robbers and necromancers, family secrets and curses, religious agonies and heresies, and repressed sexuality and violence, the first two novels take definite inspiration from the Gothic, yet *The Folly of the World* is his most overt ode to the genre yet. His short fiction, articles, and reviews have appeared in numerous magazines, anthologies, and websites, and he is editing the forthcoming anthology *Letters to Lovecraft*. He can be found physically in Colorado, and more ephemerally at www.jessebullington.com.

The Oxford Companion to English Literature describes **Ramsey Campbell** as "Britain's most respected living horror writer." He has been given more awards than any other writer in the field, including the Grand Master Award of the World Horror Convention, the Lifetime Achievement Award of the Horror Writers Association and the Living Legend Award of the International Horror Guild. Among his novels are *The Face That Must Die*, *Incarnate*, *Midnight Sun*, *The Count of Eleven*, *Silent Children*, *The Darkest Part of the Woods*, *The Overnight*, *Secret Story*, *The Grin of the Dark*, *Ghosts Know*, and *The Kind Folk*. Forthcoming are *Bad Thoughts* and *Thirteen Days* *at Sunset Beach*. His collections include *Waking Nightmares, Alone with the Horrors, Ghosts and Grisly Things, Told by the Dead*, and *Just Behind You*, and his non-fiction is collected as *Ramsey Campbell, Probably*. His regular columns appear in *Prism, Dead Reckonings*, and *Video Watchdog*, and he is the president of the Society of Fantastic Films. Ramsey Campbell lives on Merseyside with his wife, Jenny. His pleasures include classical music, good food and wine, and whatever's in that pipe. You can find him online at www.ramseycampbell.com.

S. J. Chambers writes in Florida. Her fiction has appeared in *MungBeing, Yankee Pot Roast, New Myths, Thackery T. Lambshead Cabinet of Curiosities* (Harper Voyager), and *Zombies: Shambling Through The Ages* (Prime Books). You can find her online at www.selenachambers.com.

Writer, game designer, and cad, **Richard Dansky** was named one of the Top 20 videogame writers in the world in 2009 by *Gamasutra*. His work includes bestselling games such as *Tom Clancy's Splinter Cell: Blacklist, Far Cry, Tom Clancy's Rainbow Six 3*, and *Outland*. Richard's writing has appeared in magazines ranging from *The Escapist* to *Lovecraft Studies*, as well as numerous anthologies. His most recent novel, *Vaporware*, is available from JournalStone, and he was a major contributor to White Wolf's *World of Darkness*. Richard lives in North Carolina with his wife, statistician and blogger Melinda Thielbar, and their amorphously large collections of books and single malt whiskeys.

Steve Dempsey's approach to the Gothic has been in a pale mimicry of its originator, Walpole. He is a civil servant, but sans sinecure, he lives in a modest London house rather than a romantic pile, his Grand Tour was on InterRail, not by means of carriage, and so far he has avoided the gout (although his father has done his bit to adhere to that part of the tale). Steve and his wife, Paula, are enjoying a growing reputation as writers. When they are not exploring dusty libraries, infamous caves, or the dank woods of Albion, the tapping you can hear in their dwelling is not the pipes, nor a raven at the window, but keyboards.

Laura Ellen Joyce's first novel, *The Museum of Atheism*, was published by Salt in 2012. She has had short fiction and poetry published in *Succour, Metazen, Paraxis*, and *Murmurations: An Anthology of Uncanny Stories about Birds*. Her novella *The Luminol Reels* will be published by Calamari Press in 2014. Laura teaches Literature and Creative Writing at York St John University.

Dmetri Kakmi is a writer and editor. His book *Mother Land* is probably the only memoir that features ghosts and mythological beings. *Mother Land* was shortlisted for the New South Wales Premier's Literary Awards; and is published in Australia, England, and Turkey. Dmetri also edited the acclaimed children's anthology *When We Were Young*. His essays and short stories appear in anthologies. He's currently working on two novels, one of which is a ghost story.

Damien Kelly is a writer and psychology lecturer living in the untamed wilderness of the northwest of Ireland. He's married to a beautiful pathologist and has two precocious children to fret over. The horror practically writes itself. *Season of the Macabre*, a collection of winter chillers, is published by Monico, an imprint of Clarion Publishing. You can find him online at damosays.com.

Beth K. Lewis is a Project Editor at Titan Books. A Publishing BA graduate, Beth has wide-ranging knowledge and skills in all aspects of the industry, from production to editorial. She is committed to bringing quality fiction to readers and has a particular passion for promoting debut authors. She lives in a too small flat in London with her wife and fireplace of books. Beth has had short stories published regularly since she was 13 and is working on several novels. You can find her online at bethklewis.com.

Sean Logan's stories have appeared in more than thirty publications and can be found most recently in *Black Static, Supernatural Tales, Postscripts to Darkness, Dark Visions*, and *Once Upon an Apocalypse*. He lives just north of San Francisco in a little house with a big, scary rottweiler that will run and hide at the first sign of trouble.

Ed Martin teaches English Literature in a Surrey secondary school, and often uses unsuspecting students as sounding boards for the occasional ghost story. When not teaching he can often be found exploring the Surrey countryside, searching for some interesting piece of folklore. His influences include Mervyn Peake, M. R. James, and Nigel Kneale; "The Fall of the Old Faith" is his first publication. He can be found tweeting at @EdMartin84.

Fi Michell lives in Sydney, Australia. Her love of myth, fantasy, and science fiction was born during three years of cold, rainy days in Wellington, New Zealand, as a child. She has had careers in architecture and e-commerce, but now writes whenever her two children permit. Fi Michell may be found online at http://fimichell.wordpress.com.

Phil Reeves is a British illustrator and graphic designer inspired by H. P. Lovecraft, Robert E. Howard and China Miéville. His visual work has been published by Pelgrane Press within such titles as *Sisters of Sorrow*, *Eternal Lies*, and *The Esoterrorists* 2nd Edition. In a break from his usual pursuits, in 2012 Reeves undertook writing a short story, and was praised for his "prose [being] very clean and very classic Lovecraftian gothic." He is now making plans for further fictional writing.

Mason Wild lives in a crofter's cottage overlooking the Esk valley. He shares his house with two Irish wolfhounds and a crow. He gets his ideas from a Victorian tin chest he found buried in the garden beneath a rosemary bush. This is his first published story.

Schemers

Betrayal Knows No Boundaries

A cruel lover who refashions her prey. A bioengineered warrior on the run. An internet mapping service with a stalker's eye. A carjacker with a conscience. A Victorian thespian turned super-criminal. A murderer of video game characters. All these and more meet in the poison-soaked pages of Schemers, a genre-spanning short fiction exploration of grand schemes, Machiavellian maneuvering, and the knotty, micro-scaled twistings of the human heart.

Bending genres and crossing boundaries are:

Tobias S. **BUCKELL** • Jesse **BULLINGTON** • Tania **HERSHMAN**
Ekaterina **SEDIA** • Johnathan L. **HOWARD** • Kyla Lee **WARD**
Robyn **SEALE** • Laura **LUSH** • Nick **MAMATAS** • Molly **TANZER**
John **HELFERS** • Gareth **RYDER-HANRAHAN**
Elizabeth A. **VAUGHAN** • Kathryn **KUITENBROUWER**

ISBN: 9781908983046
Available from the Stone Skin Press website
www.stoneskinpress.com

Shotguns v. Cthulhu

Pulse-pounding action meets cosmic horror in this exciting collection from the rising stars of the New Cthulhuiana. Steel your nerves, reach into your weapons locker, and tie tight your running shoes as humanity takes up arms against the monsters and gods of H. P. Lovecraft's Cthulhu Mythos. Remember to count your bullets...you may need the last one for yourself.

Relentlessly hurtling you into madness and danger are:

Natania **BARRON** • Steve **DEMPSEY** • Dennis **DETWILLER**
Larry **DiTILLIO** • Chad **FIFER** • A. Scott **GLANCY**
Dave **GROSS** • Dan **HARMS** • Rob **HEINSOO**
Kenneth **HITE** • Chris **LACKEY** • Robin D. **LAWS**
Nick **MAMATAS** • Ekaterina **SEDIA** • Kyla **WARD**

ISBN: 9781908983015
Available from the Stone Skin Press website
www.stoneskinpress.com